CARRY
ME
HOME

CARRY
ME
HOME

Janet Fox

Simon & Schuster Books for Young Readers
NEW YORK LONDON TORONTO SYDNEY NEW DELHI

SIMON & SCHUSTER BOOKS FOR YOUNG READERS
An imprint of Simon & Schuster Children's Publishing Division
1230 Avenue of the Americas, New York, New York 10020

This book is a work of fiction. Any references to historical events, real people, or real places are used fictitiously. Other names, characters, places, and events are products of the author's imagination, and any resemblance to actual events or places or persons, living or dead, is entirely coincidental.

SIMON & SCHUSTER BOOKS FOR YOUNG READERS
and related marks are trademarks of Simon & Schuster, Inc.
For information about special discounts for bulk purchases, please contact
Simon & Schuster Special Sales at 1-866-506-1949 or business@simonandschuster.com.
The Simon & Schuster Speakers Bureau can bring authors to your live event.
For more information or to book an event, contact the Simon & Schuster Speakers Bureau
at 1-866-248-3049 or visit our website at www.simonspeakers.com.
Interior design by Lizzy Bromley
The text for this book was set in Adobe Garamond Pro.
Manufactured in the United States of America
0622 FFG

2 4 6 8 10 9 7 5 3
Library of Congress Cataloging-in-Publication Data
Names: Fox, Janet S., author.
Title: Carry me home / Janet Fox.
Description: First edition. | New York, New York : Simon & Schuster Books for Young Readers, [2021] | Audience: Ages 8-12. | Audience: Grades 4-6. | Summary: Twelve-year-old Lulu, burdened with caring for her sister, Serena, since their father disappeared, must learn to trust her new friends and community when secrets and lies catch up with her.
Identifiers: LCCN 2020050899 (print) | LCCN 2020050900 (ebook)
ISBN 9781534485082 (hardcover) | ISBN 9781534485099 (paperback)
ISBN 9781534485105 (ebook)
Subjects: CYAC: Sisters--Fiction. | Homelessness—Fiction. | Abandoned children—Fiction. Friendship—Fiction. | Community life—Montana—Fiction. | Montana—Fiction.
Classification: LCC PZ7.F8342 Car 2021 (print) | LCC PZ7.F8342 (ebook)
DDC [Fic]—dc23
LC record available at https://lccn.loc.gov/2020050899
LC ebook record available at https://lccn.loc.gov/2020050900

To all children—and their parents—
who need a place to call home.
And to Jeff and Kevin,
who are my heart's home.

CARRY
ME
HOME

1
Now

THE DAY Lulu's daddy disappeared was, so far, the coldest morning of the year.

That's why she was still curled up tight under the blankets and pressed, back to warm back, against Serena when the sun shot a ray at the mirror that reflected onto Lulu's face, waking her hard. She squeezed her eyes and rubbed them, saying out loud, "What?"

She was asking the sun, *What?*

Then, "Daddy?"

Lulu sat up. The Suburban's windows were fogged and Serena stayed asleep. Their daddy was not in the back seat. His blankets were folded into squares, the way he always started his day. But today he'd started his day without waking them, without the usual rituals of wet cloth to wipe their faces, the bottle of water and toothbrush to clean their teeth, because as

Daddy had said, "No matter what, girls, we will practice good hygiene. Cleanliness is right there next to godliness."

Lulu, when he'd said this, when she was little and didn't know her words, envisioned a pair of high jeans, what she'd now call mom jeans, on a saintly figure, halo, raised eyes, with prayerful hands.

Now that she was all of twelve she knew what hygiene was. She even knew how it was spelled.

Lulu rubbed at the window as her surprise was replaced by confusion and then by a knot in her chest. Her hand made a round hole on the foggy damp glass but she couldn't see anything through the branches that encased the Suburban. Nothing moved, except the sun, which now filled the car with cold light.

It wasn't Saturday. Or Sunday. It was Thursday, a school day, and they were going to be late.

Where was Daddy? The knot tightened.

"Reenie," Lulu said, and shook her sister's shoulder. "Wake up."

Serena stirred, and her face emerged from the thicket of blankets. "Sup?"

"We're late." Lulu could tell, because it was September and the sun was at that particular slant, that they should already be well on their way. She grabbed the water bottle and wet the cloth and rubbed it rough over her face before handing it to Serena. She yanked on her sweatshirt and jeans and pushed over the seat back from the rear into the second seat where their daddy should be, then shoved the door open with her shoulder.

Man, it was chilly.

Lulu rubbed at her arms and hopped a little, foot to foot, before looking to make sure no one was able to see as she relieved herself behind the car. By the time Serena was dressed and out Lulu had cleaned her teeth and found their jackets and backpacks. She hopped foot to foot again against the shivers as she waited for Serena to finish her morning routine. "Let's go, let's go."

"I'm hungry," Serena whined. "Where's Daddy?"

"No time. Gotta go," Lulu answered. It was all she said because it was almost all she knew. Except for this.

When no one else could—could step up, could step in, could do what needed doing—Lulu would.

But.

Where was Daddy?

2

"ONLY YOUR fourth week in school, Serena Johnson, and already a tardy." The door proctor pressed her lips together as she fished out the form from her desk drawer and filled it in. "It's a bad way to start third grade."

Lulu shuffled her feet, her fingers tightening around Serena's. She wished the woman would hurry. She had to leave Serena and make her own way five minutes down the street to the middle school. Being tardy was bad enough, but now she would miss the spelling test.

Lulu had never once had a tardy in Texas. She won the school certificate for perfect attendance every single year. She pushed against the anger that she felt. Daddy had blown it today.

Where was he? What now?

She thought she'd heard him go out at some point when it

was still dark. He usually went out and used the showers and got dressed and then came back to wake them up. But not today. Today he went out and didn't come back.

When she'd left the Suburban this morning, Lulu found Daddy's wallet where he always stashed it in the well of the car door with the keys and his cell phone. There were sixty dollars and seventy-five cents in his wallet, and the cell phone was dead. She locked the car and pocketed the keys and his wallet, but left his phone, because phones weren't allowed in her middle school, plus it was dead, plus there was no one she could call.

The woman reached through the window and handed Lulu the slip, and said, "Right away, then, to her class."

"Yes, ma'am," Lulu mumbled, tugging Serena through the door and into the hall.

"I'm hungry," Serena said, her voice quiet. Lulu paused. She could've at least scrounged out a Pop Tart if she hadn't been so flustered. It made her mad at Daddy all over again.

"Go on. I'll see you at three," Lulu said. She stared at Serena's tiny back, her tattered Hello Kitty pack, the one that had been Lulu's, swaying back and forth.

Lulu ran from Serena's to her own school, got another scolding, picked up another slip, and tried not to run (running was frowned on) on the way to her homeroom.

Miss Baker put her finger to her lips as Lulu opened the door. The spelling test, almost over.

Lulu slid into her seat, catching side-eye from Deana, who wrinkled her nose as if she smelled something bad. Miss Baker said out loud, "Last word. 'Ridiculous.'"

Lulu wrote down the word, the only word on her paper, then her name, then the date, then Miss Baker's name. As they handed the papers forward, Deana, nose still wrinkled up, whispered, "Ridiculous."

Lulu's face flamed.

3
Before

AFTER ALL that badness, all the stuff that happened with Mama, all the stuff that made Lulu feel she needed to step up and do what needed doing—after all that, their daddy had tried so hard.

He tried to make it work. He tried to make their lives feel normal. Like when they were driving away, that first day on the road, the sun a purple thread in the east, the Suburban loaded.

"Now, don't you see, this car, it's pretty comfy, don't you think? We can save a ton of money."

Lulu watched his eyes as he glanced into the rearview, catching her expression. Next to her Serena stared out the window, silent, watching the post oaks and flat fields fly by. Their first day, just past dawn, the sleep crud still coating Lulu's eyelashes.

"I miss home," Serena said in a whisper.

"I know, honey," Daddy said. "But we got ourselves a road trip to better times. Right?"

A ton of quiet settled over them until Daddy said, "Hey. Did you girls know that in the olden days they used to drive cattle from Texas to Montana? So we're going right along that old trail here. I've got a tape someplace here of cattle drive songs." He fished in the storage well next to him, pulling out one tape after another until he found the one he wanted. "Good thing this old vehicle has a tape player, right? 'Cause I kept all my old tapes. We got ourselves the perfect car. The perfect home away from home." He punched the tape into the deck and a bunch of fiddles blasted out of the speakers, with harmonic men's voices singing about dogies and sagebrush.

Daddy sang along until he got both Lulu and Serena singing, too. It was one of Lulu's favorite things, singing. She loved singing even when the memories of singing made her heart hurt.

But these songs about cowboys were funny and Daddy was cheerful and Lulu forgave him in that moment because he was trying so hard to make it work.

4
Now

LULU HAD discovered that if she walked just slow enough from math to lunch she could find a table to herself.

"Honey, you're down to the last in your account," the lunch lady said. "Make sure your daddy makes another deposit before the end of next week."

Lulu nodded, eyes cast away.

She slipped into a chair and opened the milk carton, drinking the cold milk down in one long series of swallows.

"Pretty thirsty, huh?"

She opened her eyes and rubbed her hand over her mouth. The boy—Jack something, from her homeroom—sat down across from her, the silver sliding clattery on his tray as he edged it onto the table.

"What do you suppose is inside that tortilla?" Jack asked, poking at it with his knife. He glanced up at her.

Lulu shrugged, then took a bite. It wasn't bad. It wasn't good. Not Texas good. But it filled her belly. She thought about Serena, hoping she was eating a good lunch.

Jack said, "I don't like milk but they make me take it. Want mine?"

Lulu paused, mouth full. Was he okay?

She had her guard up. She could take care of herself. But there was Jack, staring at her, arm extended, cold, cold milk in that unopened container, waiting. He seemed okay.

She nodded.

"Great. 'Cause it'll just go to waste." He plopped the carton onto her tray. "You just moved into town, right? How d'you like Montana?"

Here it comes, Lulu thought. She shrugged again. "It's okay." She hesitated. She didn't want to seem too weird, saying nothing. "Kind of cold."

"Not cold yet. Just wait. Hope you've got a heavier jacket." He pointed with his fork, talking while he chewed. "Where're you from?"

Daddy had said, "It's best if we keep it to ourselves, girls. The past is the past. We're starting fresh. Just have to get our feet on the ground, that's all. Just get started."

Lulu hoped Daddy would explain where he'd been and why when he met them at after-school. She was still angry at him. But she remembered his words. "Keep it to ourselves."

"Oklahoma," Lulu answered Jack, a lie.

Jack put down his fork, and burst into song. *"O-o-o-kla-homa where the wind comes whipping down the plain,"* he sang.

The kids around them went silent, staring, then laughing. Deana said, "Ridiculous," really loud. Lulu slid halfway under the table.

"Sorry," Jack said, not sounding sorry. "I love musicals. Show tunes. I sing a lot. You must know that one, right? Since you lived there."

She didn't know that song, but she understood what he meant. Because she liked to sing, too. Just, not in the lunchroom. Not where other kids were watching. They were watching her because she had funky secondhand clothes, funky rarely cut hair, and now they were watching her because she was here with Jack who was nice but maybe a little weird. She picked up her tray, standing. "Gotta go."

"Oh. Okay." Jack gave her a bright-eyed look. "Later."

All those other eyes on her back. The sneering snide whispers. Deana saying something about smells. Then, laughing, laughing, laughing.

5
Way Before

THE HOSPITAL room was dark, except for the lights that
blinked green and red and blue and white. Lulu sat very still,
listening.

Listening to beeps. Listening to breathing. Listening to her
own heartbeat.

From the hallway she heard the whispers. She tried to hear
the words but she couldn't make them out. She wanted to
know, but then again she didn't.

She wanted to do something. Say a prayer. Make a promise. Make a wish. Anything.

She stopped trying to hear the grown-ups and began to
sing softly, a church song, a favorite song. It was the thing she
could do to feel better, to make her heartbeat slow down, to
drown out the other stuff in her head, in this room.

That was back at the beginning.

6
Now

WHEN SCHOOL ended for the day Lulu went straight to the elementary for after-school. She was the only middle-schooler who went, which was actually kind of a relief, a reprieve from those prying eyes and snide whispers. Deana was picked up by a slim woman—her mother, Lulu thought—in a brand-new black Toyota. Deana began chattering to her mom nonstop as soon as she opened the car door.

Deana seemed to still be chattering and Deana's mom looked away as the big black car—gosh, it looked a lot roomier than the Suburban, even—passed Lulu on her way to after-school.

Serena was already there, sitting with a stack of colored paper and some strange lumpy paper things scattered across the table.

"Lookie!" Serena said, holding up one of the lumps to show Lulu. "It's a dinosaur!"

"Right," said Lulu. She dropped her backpack and pulled out her English notebook.

The proctors were high school girls. They were nice enough. They gossiped and giggled in between setting up activities.

"It's called rigahmee," Serena said.

"Origami," one of the girls, Laurie, corrected. "The art of Japanese paper-folding."

Lulu bent over her work, reading a paragraph and the questions so she could write her response.

She leaned back in her chair. Huh. That was weird. She read the paragraph again, a summary of a book they were about to read. The book was about a Japanese girl who survived the Hiroshima bomb in World War II, but then developed leukemia. There was an old Japanese belief that anyone who made a thousand paper cranes by folding them in the origami way could make a wish and that wish would come true, so the girl began making paper cranes, wishing to get well.

Lulu looked up. Serena was folding a blue piece of paper. She stopped and smiled at Lulu. "See?" She held up her blue sort-of-looked-like-a-dinosaur.

At four thirty the girls began to tidy the room and ready the kids for home.

Home.

Lulu packed her homework and got Serena's things together. "Can I take this one?" Serena asked Laurie.

"Sure. Take all the ones you want."

"This one's s'posed to be a crane."

"Right," Lulu said. That one did look like a crane. "Nice work, Reenie."

If she ever once had believed in coincidences, she didn't now. Still. Weird.

They went outside to the usual spot where they'd meet Daddy. Laurie was there, coatless, waiting as the few kids and their parents came and went, her arms wrapped around her. A cold wind had begun to blow down from the mountains, and Lulu turned up the collar on her thin jacket. The wind smelled like the inside of a freezer, all dry and ice.

Daddy was not there. Lulu looked up the street one way, and looked down the other way. Anger was bubbling into something else. Into something hard that landed at the bottom of her stomach as if she'd swallowed a rock. Lulu bit her lip.

"Golly," Laurie said, rubbing her arms and jumping a little. "I think it might snow." She glanced at Lulu. "Your dad's late."

"I forgot. We're supposed to meet him at home today," Lulu lied. "I know how to get there."

"You sure?" Laurie was still hopping and seemed relieved.

"Sure," Lulu said. "Sure."

"Well, okay. See you tomorrow." Laurie beelined for the door.

"What'd you tell her that for?" Serena asked as they made their way down the street.

"Because it's cold and she wasn't wearing a coat," Lulu said. "Because I wanted to get going. Because I know the way."

Because.

No Daddy.

7

Before

"MONTANA HAS it all," Daddy said. "Mountains, rivers, lakes, forests, even wild animals."

"Wild animals?" Serena asked.

"Bears and stuff," Daddy said. Then he added, "But they're nice bears. You know. Not to worry."

Where they were at that moment had none of that. What Lulu saw, leaning against the car window as they rolled down the narrow street a week out from Texas, were drill rigs, derricks, trailers, well pumps, trucks, and flat bare land stretching as far as the eye could see in all directions.

Daddy pulled up by a trailer that was labeled WELL BOSS, and underneath that, EMPLOYMENT. "Now, you girls stay in the car for a minute, okay? I'll be right back."

Serena flopped back against the car seat. "Is he going to get us a house?"

"A job, first, I think," Lulu said. "Then a house."

Daddy was back after a time and he opened the door and got in with a sigh. He didn't turn around. "There's plenty of work for a guy like me. Trouble is, there's no place to live. They've got too many workers here and haven't built fast enough." He raised his eyes to the rearview. "You girls okay with that for a time longer? This car okay for you?"

"Sure, Daddy," Lulu said.

"Sure, Daddy," Serena echoed.

8
Now

ONE THING Daddy had for sure done right was finding this spot to park in this small Montana town. That was after they'd left the drill site. After the incident at the drill site when only Lulu was right there to stop it. After they'd driven another half a day west.

From the Suburban it was ten minutes' walk east toward school. Ten minutes' walk west to the food bank. The library and the laundromat were not far beyond the school, and the parking spot itself was well hidden in the trees to give them privacy, but they were right in the RV park, with a toilet and a washroom with showers just down the dirt road. And the RV park was fenced to keep out the bears and stuff. Until Daddy had mentioned the wild animals this was something Lulu had never thought about before.

Plus, Daddy's job here was timed now for their school

days, perfect, and it too was only a longish walk away.

They had a routine.

Saturdays they went to the food bank first, the laundromat second, and the library third. During the summer they'd spent the sunny weekday afternoons at the public pool in the park while Daddy went to work, because nobody seemed to mind two girls who might or might not have been on their own. Sundays they took drives, exploring.

Now that the girls were back in school, their weekday afternoons were short, as Daddy cooked a meal behind the Suburban while the girls showered in the RV park shower, and after dinner they went to bed with the birds.

"Bed with the birds," Daddy said. "Up with the birds and down with the birds. Healthy, wealthy, and wise." Though Lulu did use a flashlight to read herself to sleep most nights.

Daddy taught Lulu to cook on the camp stove because it was "a skill everyone should know." It was easy to use, but everything had to be put away every night because of the bears. But Daddy, handy as always, had made a sturdy box out of salvaged wood to store the stove and pots and pans and plates and silver together with the tiny little table under the Suburban.

Lulu stopped asking about a house after a while. They had what they needed for now.

They had each other.

Lulu wasn't super concerned on the day Daddy disappeared

until they got back to the Suburban and found everything just as they'd left it and still no Daddy. Now anger was mingling, stirring, like a pot of stew with worry beans thrown in.

"Lu?" Serena asked, squeezing her hand.

"For tonight we've got some peanut butter," Lulu said. "And bread. Daddy must be working an extra shift. We can manage."

After they showered and ate and before it got dark, Lulu helped Serena with the blankets—still mussed from the morning—and locked the two of them inside the car. If Daddy came back, he'd knock on the window.

"Where's Daddy?" Serena whispered.

"We're gonna be okay," Lulu said. "Go to sleep."

That night, Lulu didn't read.

9
Way Before

THE FIRST and only other time Daddy disappeared was a couple of months after the stuff with Mama was over. They were still in Texas, still in the house, still living, kind of, right down the street from angry Aunt Ruth.

Serena and Lulu, trying to be good, trying to help out, and Lulu trying not to be angry herself about all that had happened, spent more time than they would have liked at angry Aunt Ruth's house even before Daddy disappeared.

But one evening he sent Lulu and Serena home with Aunt Ruth, who was always cross, and then he up and left them, saying, "Later."

"Later" turned out to be a month.

Aunt Ruth had rules, like no talking once the lights were out. She marched around mumbling about John this and John that. Their daddy John. And she made muttering phone calls that Lulu overheard, with words that made her skin prickle.

Words like "foster" and "can't take care of them all by myself" and "send away" and "illegal."

Every night after things got quiet Serena crawled into bed with Lulu.

"Why's she so mad all the time?" Serena whispered.

Lulu thought about anger. About what that felt like. "Sometimes people who are angry are really just scared," she whispered back.

"What's she got to be scared about?"

"That Daddy won't come back."

"But, that's what I'm scared about, and I'm not angry. I'm just scared," Serena said. "Plus, that's not her scary thing. It's mine. She doesn't get to have it. She doesn't get to be scared about him not coming back." There was a choke in Serena's whispered words.

Lulu squeezed Serena's hand. "I'm here, Reenie," Lulu said. Stepping up. Stepping in. Trying to comfort Serena when comfort was scarce. Because words like "foster" and "send away" made Lulu realize there was a big, big gap that had to be filled, the kind of gap that kids could fall through when their parents weren't watching, for one reason or another. A gap that kids could fall through when grown-ups got scared. "I won't let anything bad happen."

When Daddy finally came back after that month, he was a little less sad. He had the Suburban and said something about a plan, a plan that made angry Aunt Ruth mumble and mutter even more. A plan that involved the Suburban.

Lulu was real careful not to let her daddy leave again on his own, and she stayed as far away as she could from angry Aunt Ruth, until Daddy's plan came to be.

10
Now

ON FRIDAY, through the early hours, Lulu checked the car's clock until she got up, got dressed, pulled out a couple of cold Pop Tarts, and woke Serena.

"This is really important, Reenie, so listen up," Lulu said as they were finishing the Pop Tarts. "You have to promise me."

Serena, eyes still vacant with sleepiness, just watched.

"You have to promise," Lulu said again. "Promise?"

Serena nodded.

"You can't tell anyone that Daddy's not here. Not anyone. No kids. No adults. Nobody."

"Where is he?" Serena asked, her voice a tremolo.

Lulu's left hand was behind her back. She clenched that fist. "If you tell someone, they'll separate us. They'll take us away. We won't be together. Understand?" She'd heard enough of those words at angry Aunt Ruth's, enough to know the truth of things, enough to know what adults did with kids like Lulu and Serena who didn't have adults around.

Plus, Daddy had said, "Let's keep it a secret, okay, Lu? Some folks just don't understand certain things, like us living out here," and he'd pointed around the RV park. "Some folks think it might be bad for you girls. But I'm taking care of you, Lulu. That's not bad, is it? We're together. And that's not bad."

And it wasn't, until now.

Serena let out a little sob. "But where's Daddy?"

Lulu tightened that clenched fist. "They don't let little kids be alone. They'll take you to one place and me to another. Maybe even take one of us back to Aunt Ruth. Or to someone worse. Is that what you want?" Lulu didn't want to sound mean, but she had to make Serena understand.

Serena shook her head, her eyes growing wide.

"Okay, then. It's okay. I know what to do. I'm gonna take care of everything like I did before. You know that, right?"

Serena nodded.

Lulu smiled, tight. She said, "I can even cook and stuff. I know what to do until Daddy comes back."

"Daddy's coming back?"

"Of course he is." Of course. Lulu's fisted hand was now crossed fingers, crossed for both a promise and a lie.

When they got to the elementary school, Lulu took ten dollars from the wallet and gave it to the door proctor. "For Serena Johnson's lunches," she said.

The woman looked from the ten-dollar bill to Lulu's face. "Where's your father?"

"Working extra," Lulu said. She met the woman's eyes straight on. "'Cause, you know, we need some warmer coats." Serena's hand, interlocked in hers, was icy cold. It was gray and blustery outside.

The woman took the money. Then she said, her voice soft, "Over at the Lutheran church they do a coat drive every fall. It's tomorrow. Coats are free to those who need them."

Lulu's heart lifted. "Thanks."

11

JACK PLUNKED the milk onto Lulu's tray without asking. She looked at it for a minute, considering. Daddy would've said, "It's a sin to waste good food." She reached for the milk.

"I'm trying out for the lead," he said.

"Sorry?" Lulu asked.

"*Schoolhouse Rock.* The musical. The auditions are next week."

"Oh!" Lulu slowly opened the milk carton, then sipped.

"Do you like to sing?"

Lulu regarded Jack. "Yeah. I do. I can sing." She wasn't going to go overboard. She still hardly knew him, just knew that he gave her his milk.

"Great! Why don't you try out, too? I know all the songs. I can teach you. Even if you don't sing great, it's the kind of musical you can fake. Plus, you can sing any song for the audition, just to show them."

"I can sing," Lulu repeated, soft.

"Want my help? What're you doing this weekend? I could come by your house—"

"Can't this weekend." Or any weekend.

Jack chewed his pizza. "Okay. Maybe next week? Like, one afternoon after school?"

"Yeah. Maybe." The milk was nice and cold. Lulu concentrated on the milk.

12

Before

THEY'D ONLY been there a few days, in that flat-land drilling place with all those men and almost no women and no children. A week on the road from Texas just to be there, "where the work was," Daddy said. With the pump jacks and well diggers and oily smells and no homes for families.

Lulu hated the place. It was hot, dry, dusty, and filled with big men who smelled bad. Daddy had had to park the Suburban in a bare lot, squeezed between a couple of giant RVs that hummed, loud, day and night.

"The pay is real good," Daddy said. "Real good. We won't have to be here too long before we have good money. Maybe just be here for the summer." He'd started to smell bad, too. There were no showers for those without RVs. Just stinky port-o-potties.

He worked long hours, up at dawn and not back until well

after dark. Lulu was starting to learn from Daddy how to cook a bit on the camp stove, but she and Serena were bored out of their minds. They hated spending those long hot days inside the stuffy car.

That's how it happened.

Lulu was reading, lying on her back on the tailgate, blanket under her head, headphones in her ears. The RVs hummed. Serena was playing in the dirt out away from the Suburban with the Barbie she'd brought from home. Next thing Lulu knew Serena was no longer saying stuff in a made-up dialogue barely audible over the hum and the music in her headphones.

Lulu sat up. Barbie was splayed facedown in the dust ten feet away.

"Reenie?" Lulu called. She hopped off the tailgate. "Serena?"

There, way down the street, really far down the street, so far Lulu was shocked, was tiny Serena, holding the hand of a large man who walked super fast, kind of dragging Lulu's sister, his back to Lulu, Serena trying to look back at the Suburban, the man making for a rusty van that was parked out by the Stop-N-Go but left running, its tailpipe spewing.

Lulu didn't pause to close up the car or pick up Barbie.

When she reached them Lulu's side ached and she couldn't talk. She grabbed for Serena's free hand. The big man whirled and held on tight to Serena's other.

"Lu?" Serena said in a tiny scared voice.

"Let go. Let go!" the man said, yanking.

"No!" Lulu managed. Then, "Help!"

A woman in front of the store turned on the sidewalk, lifting her hand to shade her eyes. "Hey," she called. "What's going on there?"

The man dropped Serena's hand, made for the van, and once in, roared away.

When Lulu told Daddy later he didn't move for a long minute. Then he reached for Lulu and Serena and pulled them to his chest; Lulu could feel his whole body shaking. She didn't care about the smell. She held on to her daddy and her sister so tight it hurt.

By dawn they were on their way.

"West," Daddy said, not meeting Lulu's eyes in the rear-view. "It'll be nicer a bit west."

13
Now

SATURDAY, TWO days after Daddy disappeared, the sun came out. The peaks were topped by a dusting of new snow but the mountainsides were still bare, browning up with autumn, with dots of gold and red from the aspen and chokecherries. Lulu knew the Saturday routine. She knew the routes except the one to get to the Lutheran church, but the church couldn't be far. Not in this small town.

Lulu had to stick to the routine. Step up. Step in. Take care of herself and most especially of Serena, like she had at the drill site. Then maybe Daddy would come back, just like he had last time, back in Texas. When he'd gone last time, she'd stepped up and taken care of herself and Serena.

When he got back this time, he'd be so proud of Lulu.

If he wasn't back by Monday, she could go looking for him, although she didn't really know where she'd start. Perhaps she'd find someone he worked with. Maybe he'd said something to the guys he worked with about going somewhere. She didn't know enough about any of the adults around to trust any of them not to take her and Serena someplace they didn't want to be. But she'd sort it out later, because right now she could step up.

Right now it was Saturday, and she knew what to do. They had their routine.

The first stop was the food bank, because it opened bright and early. Daddy had found a discarded shopping cart they'd used all summer and Lulu pushed while Serena skipped beside her. Lulu loaded up the cart with all the things Daddy usually got, plus they had some fresh salad greens and carrots, which Daddy didn't like but Lulu thought were important. And she got an extra milk.

They dropped the food off in the car cooler before heading for the laundromat and the library, having traded out the food for the laundry.

After the laundromat Lulu parked the shopping cart carrying their now-clean clothes just inside the library door. Ms. Maurene was at the desk in the children's section, as usual on Saturdays.

"Can you tell me please where I might find the Lutheran church?" Lulu asked.

Ms. M fished around in a drawer at her desk and pulled

out a town map. "We're here, okay? The Lutheran church is right there. About four blocks west. You going to the coat drive?"

Lulu's cheeks went hot.

"It's okay, hon. Lots of people who are new to Montana discover they don't have warm enough coats. You get the warmest you can, okay?"

Lulu nodded.

"Your dad all right? I saved him yesterday's paper. I know he likes to read the news from time to time."

Lulu nodded again, looking hard at Serena, who chewed her lip. Lulu took the newspaper and folded it in thirds.

She and Serena picked out four books apiece and Ms. M checked them out. Lulu had been so happy when Daddy had used the RV park address so they could get library cards, even though they never got mail. "Just for you, Lulu, 'cause you love to read."

"Say, Lulu?" Ms. M said.

Lulu turned.

"I'm thinking about setting up a corner in the laundromat with books for kids. I talked to the owner and she said it was fine with her. But I need a little help choosing the right books. Most of the kids who spend time there are your age or a little younger. You think you could help me with that?"

Lulu tried not to register her surprise.

"You're a regular here since spring and I thought you'd have a pretty good idea what might work. Start thinking about it, okay?"

Lulu gave Ms. M a big smile. "Okay."

14

LULU SAT behind the wheel of the Suburban. She counted the money again and did a little mental math. She'd paid for two weeks of Serena's and her own school lunches. She'd paid for the laundry. That left her with thirty-five dollars and seventy-five cents.

The slip of paper that was tucked under the windshield wiper while they were at the laundromat said that they owed twenty dollars to the RV park for the next week's rent, cheaper now that fall had arrived and the RV park was half empty, or so the note said, with a smiley face at the end.

She snuggled inside her big new coat. Well, new to her, but definitely big. There was a whole rack of large puffy gently used (so the sign said) kids' coats. Serena wanted a blue coat but it was already a little small, so Lulu convinced her to choose the bright pink coat that would fit for at least a year.

Lulu's coat was black, and though she thought it was kind of ugly, like a stack of inner tubes wrapping around her body, it sure was warm. The ladies at the church didn't ask them any questions, and one even fished out a couple of knitted hats from a bag at her feet.

"I made these myself," she said, proud.

Serena had pulled her hat straight down to her eyebrows and grinned at the woman.

"My, you are a pretty little thing. So sweet, why, I could just eat you up," she said to Serena, which prompted Lulu to take Serena's hand tight and leave without a thank-you.

Now she felt bad about not thanking the ladies.

She had to start dinner. This was her first time cooking on the camp stove all by herself, but the only healthy food they had, other than peanut butter, needed to be heated up, so she did. And it wasn't so bad, with one of the prepackaged meals from the food bank plus some carrots. Serena didn't complain.

Lulu decided she'd make extra so she didn't have to cook for a couple of nights. And maybe extra so if Daddy came home tonight he'd be able to eat. Maybe he'd come home. It was a Saturday, after all. And the day they usually all spent together.

He must be hungry, wherever he was. He must be. Because he didn't have his wallet, so how could he eat? Even if he was somewhere else, in some other town, in a shelter, for a reason she couldn't possibly know, he wouldn't just fill himself up on food and not be thinking about Lulu and Serena.

That other time he'd disappeared, he'd left them with Aunt Ruth. This time he'd disappeared and left them alone. Last time he'd come back with the Suburban and a plan. So, was he about to come back with a new car? A new plan?

Last time he'd left out of sheer overwhelming sadness. As Daddy put it, "an inability to cope." Is that what happened this time?

Daddy had to be okay . . . Lulu wasn't going to think about any other possibility. He had to be out there somewhere, thinking about them, and thinking about getting back to them, and because she was sure he wouldn't eat without thinking about them, he'd be hungry.

Lulu wasn't so hungry herself in this moment, with her mind chewing on everything. Chewing on Daddy's disappearance, on his sadness, and especially on her wish that he'd come back, right now.

It was hard, this responsibility. Hard to cook. Hard to eat. Hard to keep to the routine. Hard to worry about Serena, about Daddy. Hard to worry about money. Hard.

Hard without Daddy.

But. Lulu would stand up.

Now Lulu would have to think about the money. All she had of any value besides her music player and headphones was Daddy's dead cell, and he'd long ago lost the battery charger.

"Don't need that old phone anyway, do we, Lu," he'd said. "This way your aunt can't bother us."

Maybe she could sell a dead phone to someone who wouldn't mind buying a charger. But for now, after paying this week's RV park rent, she'd have fifteen dollars and seventy-five cents left in the wallet. That would only last until the next weekend, for anything that might come up, and then she'd have to pay the RV park again and she wouldn't have enough. She had to believe that Daddy would show up before that fifteen dollars and seventy-five cents was gone. Before the next rent note. Before the next school lunch was due.

Before something else bad happened that she couldn't predict, something fated to happen.

Lulu knew for almost certain that there were no coincidences. But there sure was fate.

15
Before

HANGING OVER the kitchen table in the house in Texas, the house that was their home until it wasn't, was a pale yellow glass ball. Lulu had done homework night after night by the light of that glass ball, while her mother cleaned up after dinner. Lulu and Serena had done jigsaw puzzles by the light of that glass ball, while music played on the radio. Lulu's daddy had read the newspaper by the light of that glass ball, occasionally remarking to Lulu's mother on one thing or the other.

The night that Lulu had heard a noise when she was supposed to be sleeping—about six months before they left Texas and not long before Daddy had disappeared that first time—she'd snuck down the stairs, stood in the dark hallway, and looked at the kitchen table that was lit by that glass ball. The table was piled with papers, stacks and stacks of them. Daddy sat at the table with his head in his hands, and Lulu realized what the noise was.

Daddy was sobbing, a wailing, grieving sound. She knew the word for it. Keening.

She'd only seen her daddy cry once before. Not very long before, either.

Lulu bit her cheek so hard she tasted blood; she was not going to cry.

Not then. Nope. Not ever, ever, ever.

16
Now

ON SUNDAY, Lulu decided they had to go back to the Lutheran church. That was not the kind of church they used to go to in Texas, but for one thing Lulu knew where the Lutheran church was now and for another she felt obliged to go back and say thank you to the ladies who ran the coat drive. She found the service times in the newspaper Ms. M had given her.

Church-going had stopped after Mama. Daddy said he just couldn't go and listen to the choir without her singing. But really, Lulu had the feeling that Daddy was too angry at God to go back to church. She'd heard it herself, heard her daddy in the dark of night, saying "Why? Why?" and Lulu was sure her daddy wasn't talking to himself. Then they'd gotten the Suburban and left Texas and had a very different routine from before, and because Daddy seemed happier, that was okay with Lulu.

She and Serena sat in the back pew and listened politely to everything. When it was time to pray Lulu prayed so hard she thought the prayers would explode her brain. She hadn't prayed in a long time, so she wondered whether God would remember her. She could feel Serena next to her, praying even harder.

Lulu knew that Serena was praying for the same thing she was. Big, big prayers, so big she felt very small. So big she had to beg to let God know that they were really important, and please couldn't God help, even just a tiny little bit, even if Lulu had disappeared from praying for a time?

Please let him come back. Please make it today. Please. Please. Please. Please. Please.

She squeezed her eyes tight so nothing that might have snuck past her guarded wall could sneak out.

But when it came time to sing the hymns, Lulu found her way into the hymnal and picked up the tune and sang. She sang loud. She pushed the music right out through her heart. It was comforting, a release.

At the end of the service a young couple sitting in front of Lulu and Serena turned around.

"You have a lovely voice," the woman said to Lulu. She bounced a gurgling baby in her arms.

Her husband nodded. "I hope you'll think about joining the choir."

Lulu said, "Um, we're not members or anything. Just visiting."

"Just visiting," Serena echoed. She reached up and played with the baby's foot, and began making faces at the baby and gurgling noises, too.

"I hope you sing somewhere," the man said.

"Lovely voice," the woman said. "You should come more often."

The Lutherans put out a breakfast after the service and Lulu had to keep reminding Serena to eat slowly. "You don't want them to think we're starving," she whispered.

"But I am starving," Serena said, and went back for another sticky sweet roll.

As they left Lulu recognized the woman from the coat drive. She told Serena they needed to be polite to that nice lady.

"Thank you for the coats. And the hats," Lulu said. "The hats are really nice."

"Oh! Well." She beamed at them, glancing from Lulu to Serena and back. "You're welcome. I'm glad you like them." She peered behind the girls. "Are your parents here?"

Serena looked at Lulu, who gave her sister "the look" back.

But Serena must have wanted to answer in some way to be polite. "Our mom's—" Serena began.

Lulu interrupted. "Got to go."

She dragged Serena down the street as fast as she could. "Don't," Lulu said. Serena whimpered as they went and Lulu felt terrible. But she couldn't bear to hear the words said out loud and that felt even more terrible. "Don't ever say that. Don't ever."

17

Before

EVERY SUNDAY after they'd moved to this Montana town, instead of going to church, Daddy drove the Suburban around "to keep the battery alive." He edged carefully out of their spot, drove slowly out of the RV park, and slowly down the main road and even up the back roads. That was how Lulu had come to know the town better.

They drove up to the mountains where Daddy showed them a river so clear they could see each rock on the bottom, and even saw fish, lying long and low on the bottom, waiting for food. He showed them how to catch a fish, which he had done a lot as a boy and was excited to do again now, and he would have showed them how to cook the fish and have it for supper if Serena hadn't burst into tears and begged him to put the fish back in the stream.

He said, "It's okay, Reenie. It's called catch and release. I'll just release him right back and he'll be fine. Free." He patted Serena's head. "Like us."

Daddy showed them the plants he knew and the ones he didn't, that Lulu later looked up in the library. They walked up the trails through the wildflowers and rocks and under the wide blue sky until Serena complained. He showed them antelope, and together they sang that song they'd sung as they were driving up from Texas.

They saw deer and more antelope and even a fox, but they didn't see any bears, which made Lulu feel a whole lot better, but Serena was disappointed and said so.

Daddy showed them the nice houses that had pretty gardens and big old trees in the middle of the old part of town. He had shown them where they'd be going to school. He showed them the hospital, "in case," but Lulu always looked out the other window.

And he showed them where he was working, a short street at the far east end of town with a dozen houses in various stages of being built.

"I just finished framing that one," he said proudly, in August, pointing to a small two-story that was framed and roofed and about to be weathered in. "About to start on the one next door."

"Is that gonna be our house, Daddy?" Serena said, unable to keep the excitement out of her voice.

He waited a long time before answering. "Not that one, honey. But I'm working on it. We'll get there."

18

Now

By the time they got back to the car after this Sunday service the day had warmed considerably. They changed out their coats from the heavy Lutheran ones to their light Texas jackets.

"Indian summer," Lulu said.

"Native American summer," Serena corrected. "Or, I think what we're supposed to say is ingenious summer."

"It's just an expression, Indian summer," Lulu said. "And not ingenious," she corrected.

"Yeah, but my teacher talks about being thoughtful about Native Americans 'cause they were here first after all and to not have Columbus Day and stuff. So it's ingenious. Not Indian."

"Indigenous. Not ingenious." Lulu smiled. "Let's go for a walk."

"K."

She remembered from their Sunday drives the way to Daddy's workplace, to that small new neighborhood on the far east end of town. They walked east in the sunlight, Lulu tilting her head back every once in a while to pick up the birdsong and smell the autumn air. Kids rode by on bicycles, and people were out in their yards raking leaves. The sun was warm on the top of her head. Her long braid was hot on her back.

She was so homesick, all of a sudden, seeing all those families at their homes, that it hurt like the dickens.

She wanted Daddy so much it hurt even more. She wanted to be able to beg him to get in the Suburban and drive them home to the house in Texas. The mountains were pretty. But she missed missed *missed* that yellow glass globe light and that kitchen and that living room and her own bedroom with her own bed and she missed so much more that she didn't want to think about; her stomach ached with missingness.

The sunlight blinked and winked and made Lulu's eyes smart.

It took a while to get to the development, and the street with those new-built houses was quiet. A couple of houses were finished and even lived in, the sod just settling, the trees still tiny, but no one was about.

Then Lulu heard the pop of a nail gun. She and Serena made for it, Lulu's heart pounding.

It wasn't Daddy.

"Hey," Lulu said loud. It was time to try and find out something.

The man looked down as they looked up.

"Do you know John Johnson?" Lulu asked.

The man looked at them for a long minute. "Hasn't been around for a few days." He paused. "You his kids?"

Lulu put her guard up, hard and fast. "Oh, no. No. Just neighbors. That's all. Just being neighborly. Seeing if he's around." Wishing that he was around. But he wasn't.

"I haven't seen him for a couple of days. Not like him to miss work."

"Oh," Lulu said. It was all she could think to say and not let down her wall. She didn't know this man. As Daddy had said, "Let's just keep it to ourselves, girls."

"Talented guy. Good worker. Bragged about his kids. Two girls, about your ages." He paused, pushing his gimme cap back and wiping his brow. "Said they were real smart."

Lulu swallowed.

"I'm Hank. His boss. You see him, you tell him he's still got the job. Real good worker."

"Okay," Lulu said.

The man hesitated. "He left his tool bag," he said, and pointed. "Usually left it overnight when we lock up but it's been here all weekend. Not like him."

Lulu walked over to her daddy's tool bag. The canvas was pocked with small holes and bulged with the odd shapes of hammers, screwdrivers, and pliers, and even a couple of expensive tools like electric drills.

She could say something to this man, Hank, her daddy's boss, right now. She could tell him the truth. But she didn't know him. He was another grown-up who might or might not stand up and do the right thing.

But Lulu would stand up, as she already had.

Her daddy was very attached to his tools. He wouldn't leave them just lying around like that all weekend. That was so unlike him. So unlike.

"A guy's got to have his tools," Hank said, echoing Lulu's thoughts. "Why don't you take the bag to him? Since you know him? Since you're neighbors and all. Think you can carry it?"

"Sure," Lulu said. She picked it up, hefting it in both hands. "Bye."

She didn't hear the nail gun start up again until they turned the corner back toward town and the RV park on the other side of town. Then she walked as fast as she could considering the super heavy tool bag and Serena's slow pace. By the time they got back to the Suburban her arms ached like nobody's business.

19

Jack almost dropped his tray on Lulu's head, but he managed to finesse the move at the last minute. "Whoa. Sorry. That was close." He plucked the milk from his own tray and put it on Lulu's. "They gave me an extra dessert. Want it?"

Lulu hesitated, then nodded. Deana, having seen the near-catastrophe from her seat at the next table, was giggling, pointing, whispering. Lulu looked away.

"So, tomorrow, after school, how about we rehearse for the auditions?" Jack yanked a piece of paper from his back pocket and put it down in front of Lulu.

Tryouts! it read. *Join the fun at* Schoolhouse Rock The Musical*! Be part of the team! Just bring your best singing voice and dancing feet. 4PM Friday. Gym.*

"I can't dance," Lulu said, looking up at Jack.

"No problemo," Jack said. "I can show you a few steps. But

like you said, you can sing? Awesome." He ate as if he'd never eaten before. "I like your new coat," he said with his mouth full.

"What?" she said, not able to understand the words.

"The new coat. I saw you in it this morning. It'll be good all winter. Especially come February. It's the wind around here that'll get you. So that coat's perfect."

"Oh. That's good." He'd seen her in the new coat. Did he walk to school, too? She didn't want to be seen coming from where she was coming from.

"So, tomorrow, we can get together when the bell rings at the end of the day and I'm pretty sure the gym will be empty and we can rehearse. Okay?"

"Okay," Lulu said. Music. Singing. She'd been so happy singing those hymns. She'd forgotten how happy singing made her. "Okay."

She smiled and Jack smiled back.

As she left school for after-school, she heard Deana say behind her back, "She looks like the Michelin Man. You know, the one who's made out of tires." Deana was wearing something sleek and form-fitting with fake fur insides. She looked like a princess.

The other girls with Deana laughed.

20

THEY WERE back to making origami animals in after-school. This time, when Lulu had finished her homework, she asked Laurie to show her how to make a paper crane.

"Oh, so you know the story, right?" Laurie asked while she showed Lulu the folds. "We read it in middle school, too. The thousand paper cranes that girl made? That's a lot of cranes. But the legend goes that's what you need to make a wish come true, one thousand of them. Except that she died, poor thing. Leukemia. Aftermath of the Hiroshima atomic bomb."

Lulu thought a thousand paper cranes was a lot, too, especially after she started trying to make her own. Then she thought—and shoved aside—the idea that wishes might not come true. That Sadako did not survive. Lulu buried that idea right under the table where she sat next to her sister. Because wishes should come true.

"This is hard." Lulu set her first messy attempt to the right of her new sheet of colored paper.

"You'll get the hang of it. Let's go more slowly. Oh, and if you do this at home, you need squares of paper, not rectangles or anything else. Here." Laurie handed Lulu a whole stack of brightly colored paper.

Lulu slipped the stack of paper into her backpack. A stack of wishes, waiting to be made.

By the end of after-school Lulu had succeeded in making one marginally okay green paper crane. One thousand, she thought once more, was a lot of cranes.

"Your dad not here again?" Laurie asked. Today she was also wrapped in a bigger, warmer coat.

"They changed his hours," Lulu lied.

"But Lulu knows how to get home from here," Serena piped up. Lulu looked down and smiled.

"Okay, I guess. Technically, I'm not supposed to let you go without a parent," Laurie said. "I could get in a lot of trouble." She paused. "Maybe you could bring me a note from him? Saying it's okay?"

A pit opened in Lulu's stomach. "Sure." Then she remembered. "Oh, but tomorrow I won't be in after-school. I'll be picking up Serena at four."

"Why?" Serena asked, face turned up.

"Play rehearsals," Lulu said.

"Play rehearsals?" Serena echoed.

"Okay," said Laurie, making for the door. "But be sure to bring that note from your dad, okay?"

The pit widened.

Cooking dinner was really hard now that it had gotten cold. It was hard to start the camp stove. The wind would pick up at the wrong time and blow out the fire. Lulu needed her big coat against the chill but it was so puffy it made it hard for her to move, hard for her to scrunch down next to the stove. Some nights she didn't bother to shower, between the cold and the effort of making dinner.

"Beans and rice again?" Serena groaned. "Can't you make something else?"

"I'll do hot dogs tomorrow," Lulu said. "But tonight that's all we have." She tried not to sound snappish but she kept going back to that note she had to produce from their missing daddy.

In the darkness, when she heard Serena's soft breathing, she pulled at her backpack and felt around and found the green paper crane. She held it up in two fingers against the dim light coming from outside the car.

A wish. A thousand cranes.

It did look like a bird, that green paper crane, in the shadows, as a silhouette. It did look like a crane. A thousand paper cranes was a lot to have to make for just one wish. But she'd started with one, as everyone did.

One wish. One crane. Start with the first.

It was such a big wish, Lulu's wish.

Right then, that's what Lulu knew she needed. She had to make those cranes. In her spare minutes when she could, she'd make a thousand paper cranes. She could pray, sure, like she had in church, but this was something she could *do*, with her own two hands. Because she had to make her wish come true.

But what if her wish was so huge, so ginormous, that even one thousand paper cranes wouldn't do the trick? What would it take? Two thousand? Ten thousand? This big ginormous wish that felt impossible because it was so desperate?

What would it take?

21
Way Before

LULU KNEW that some people cried a lot. And some people didn't.

Her second-grade teacher, Miss Walton, cried when she laughed, and she cried when she read something beautiful out loud, and she cried when one of her students cried. She cried when she was happy. She cried when she was sad. She cried when she was given a thank-you card. She told the class she cried at a TV holiday special, and she cried at the evening news.

One day on the playground, Miss Walton stopped all the kids who were hollering and running around and gathered them together and pointed to the sky. The sandhill cranes were flying overhead, returning to the north country from their winter in Brazoria in Texas. There were hundreds, maybe thousands of giant birds, calling and crying their warbling chant. All the kids, even the rough and tumble, were speech-less.

"They go as far north as Canada," Miss Walton said in a soft voice. "They fly in such large numbers, like a giant family, a social group. They do that for survival. For each other. Listen to their call. Just listen. Like they're keening." When Lulu looked her way, Miss Walton was crying. Miss Walton cried a lot.

Lulu looked the word up later. Keening was the action of wailing in grief.

Lulu was not someone who cried. She wasn't sure why. Sometimes her chest hurt with keeping the crying locked inside, but lots of times she just didn't want to cry. So she didn't, even when others did.

Lulu didn't cry when her daddy told them about mama being sick. She didn't cry later, either, when it got worse. She didn't cry when she and Serena stayed that month with Aunt Ruth, and she didn't cry when Daddy packed them up in the Suburban and left Texas.

Crying just wasn't her way.

22
Now

MISS BAKER handed out preliminary grades the next morning. When she came to Lulu she said in a soft voice, "You would have an A except for that missing test."

She meant the test that Lulu hadn't made up like she could have after school because she'd been too busy taking care of Serena.

The test that she'd missed because she was late, last Thursday. The disappearance morning. Now it was six days later and still no Daddy.

Six hard days.

Lulu was angry again, really angry. And then, she realized, she was scared.

That made her think about angry Aunt Ruth, still living in the house down the street from Lulu's old house. Lulu wondered whether Aunt Ruth was worried about Lulu and Serena, since they hadn't said good-bye when they left early, early in the morning, as that was part of the plan. They'd locked the door to the mostly empty house with the yellow globe light, and driven away with Daddy in the Suburban, leaving it all behind.

Leaving Aunt Ruth behind. Angry, scared, worried Aunt Ruth.

Angry, scared, worried Lulu.

Daddy hadn't ever said what to do if he went missing again. Instead, he'd said, "It won't happen again, Lu."

Well, it had. And just like when he'd gone missing the first time, Lulu had been stepping up, but this time it was harder and scarier, because back then at least she'd been in a house even if the house had been angry Aunt Ruth's.

How much longer? When should she tell someone? When would he come back to them? When?

And who? Who could she trust? Who could she lean on? Was it enough to make a wish, to make a thousand paper cranes?

How could she find answers to all these questions?

Where are you?

23

AFTER SCHOOL on Tuesday Lulu met Jack in the hallway.

"C'mon," Jack said, leading the way.

The gym was deserted, and Lulu parked her backpack and coat on a chair before following Jack slowly up the stairs to the stage.

"It's my first time on a stage," Lulu said. "It feels . . . weird." All that empty space. "How does it work? I mean, where's the audience?"

"They've got chairs and stuff that they put up for the performance. Now, when you do the tryouts, you'll have a mic and the three teachers will be sitting right there." Jack pointed. "It's important to know that because you don't want to look at them."

"I don't?"

"You want to look right up there." He pointed to the back

wall where the plaques to the winning basketball teams hung.

"Why?"

"It'll make you feel less nervous," he said. Then he shrugged. "That's what I do, anyhow. Plus, once the lights are on you in the performance, you won't be able to see the audience. So you practice looking back there."

Lulu turned to Jack. "How often have you done this?"

Jack smiled. "I've wanted to be in theater since I was five."

"Wow."

"But you can sing."

"In my bedroom. In church," Lulu said. "But . . ."

"You'll be fine. Okay, then. What's your song?"

"Pardon?"

"What're you going to sing? You can sing whatever you want. Though I recommend a show tune."

"Oh. Right." Lulu hesitated, thinking about the songs that she knew. "What if I don't know any show tunes?"

"Then, try something upbeat. Like . . . ," and Jack hummed something Lulu had never heard before.

The song that popped into Lulu's mind then was definitely not a show tune. And it wasn't upbeat in the way Jack meant. But it was hopeful.

And she knew it by heart. She'd hummed it in her mother's hospital room. She'd sung it endlessly after her mother . . . Over and over, as if it could've saved her from something dark. Over and over and over. And ever since.

"Okay. I know something." Lulu cleared her throat.

She closed her eyes. She began to sing, so soft at first she could barely hear herself. She slipped inside the song, deep, quiet, a hymn, but hers. With each word her voice grew. With each word the song echoed until it filled the room.

'Tis the gift to be simple, 'tis the gift to be free
'Tis the gift to come down where we ought to be,
And when we find ourselves in the place just right,
'Twill be in the valley of love and delight.

"Whoa!" Jack said "Whoa!"

"What?" Lulu's eyes shot open, the dream interrupted. She was horrified. What had she done?

He stood, facing her, his arms outstretched. "You . . . your voice . . . that is . . . I'm sorry. I mean, I couldn't help it. You sound like, you sound like, like . . ." Jack flopped around the stage like he couldn't stop. And then he began to dance. "Like this!" he shouted. And his flopping turned into something else.

He danced with grace and with pure joy. He danced.

It was magic.

Like a dream.

Lulu had never seen anyone dance like that. Like he could fly. Like he meant it. Like he couldn't not dance. He was graceful, his arms and legs stretched as if they were fluid. He was on point, pulling himself together and up and up, tighter and tighter, then releasing like a spring. Turning, turning, turning.

She began to sing again, and he danced to her song.

When she finished the song, he finished the dance. She and Jack stopped, and faced each other on the stage, staring. He was panting. She was breathless.

He straightened. "Okay, then."

"Okay."

They picked up their things. Lulu felt as if she'd just been to the moon and back.

As they turned out the lights to the gym Lulu thought she caught a flutter of movement behind the stage curtain, but when she looked again the stage was bare and still.

They reached the door to the outside world.

"You'll be good. For Friday."

She nodded.

"Listen, we could try that again. That same deal. I mean, if you want. At the tryouts. Friday. You sing, I dance." Jack's face was flushed. His eyes shone bright.

She nodded again, hugging her backpack to her chest. "I'd like that."

24

LULU WAS late to after-school. Serena was in tears.

Lulu tried to hug her but Serena pulled away and put her head down on the table and sobbed. Her shaking head was haloed by origami creatures.

"Look," Laurie said. "I really need to speak with your dad." She had her hands on her hips.

Lulu nodded.

"Like, tomorrow."

"He's sick."

Laurie squinted. "As in . . ."

"Flu. He's got the flu. So he's home in bed and can't come."

"Can he write?"

"He's really sick."

Laurie threw her hands in the air. "I'm sorry. Sorry he's sick. Don't be late tomorrow. They're gonna have my head. I don't do this job for kicks. You know this is for college credits, right?"

Lulu said, soft, "I didn't know."

"Well, it is, and if I get a bad report because one of my students is not being properly taken care of, it could mean I don't get credit."

"I'm sorry," Lulu said.

"Whatever." Laurie's face was flushed, and she put her hand on Serena's head, smoothing her hair. Serena stopped sobbing and settled. "I hope your dad feels better. I really do. But please get me that note."

Lulu bent and retrieved Serena's pack and shoveled her origami creations—birds, frogs, dogs—inside. "C'mon, Reenie. It's okay."

Serena got up, shrugging off Lulu's touch, but she went with her out the door and down the street.

Twilight was falling. Late September. The days were short and getting shorter.

Halfway back to the RV park Serena said, her voice choked with tears, anger, and, yes, fear, "It's not okay. It's not okay at all."

25
Before

THE FIRST yard sale was for the big stuff. The TV, sofa, dining set, that kind of thing. Extras. What seemed like extras. Especially later.

Daddy sat at the kitchen table that night counting the money. Aunt Ruth sat next to him, tallying against the bills.

"There's no way, John. This isn't even—"

"Ruth. Not in front of the girls."

Aunt Ruth turned. Lulu stared her straight in the eye. Aunt Ruth's gaze narrowed to slits. "You girls should be asleep. With no talking."

The second yard sale was a little more of a challenge, but Lulu treated it like an Easter egg hunt. Find just the right thing. Put it on the table in the garage with a sticky tag. Price it just right.

The third yard sale was when Aunt Ruth took Serena to

the mall so Lulu could sell most of the toys. When they came home Serena had a meltdown.

Daddy sat at the kitchen table under the yellow globe light and stared down at the tabletop, still littered with piles of papers. That table and the three chairs around it were about the only things left in the house besides the mattresses. The house sounded hollow, like a drum, so Serena's cries were amplified.

"John, I told you. They're going to take the house. They'll come after you—"

Daddy stood up and said to Lulu, "You and Reenie go with Auntie Ruth, now. To her house, now. I'll come get you later." Daddy's eyes were so bright they were practically headlights.

Aunt Ruth, her own eyes narrow slits, said, "Now, wait just a minute—"

Daddy kissed Lulu's head and added one more word. "Later." Then he walked out of the house. His truck screeched away.

When he came back after a month, he was driving the Suburban; his truck was gone. The Suburban was maybe ten years older than the truck and had some rusty patches. But he acted like it was the best vehicle in the world. He acted like everything was back to normal. He'd bought the Barbie for Serena, secondhand, but in decent shape.

Aunt Ruth stood in the front yard, her arms folded tight over her chest as Daddy hugged the girls over and over. Serena wouldn't let go of his leg as he hobbled around pointing out the high points of his new vehicle.

"Will you look at that classic? Only eighty thousand miles on that baby. And wait'll you see what I've made inside." He'd tricked out the car with a kind of sleeping place for Lulu and Serena in the back, and a place for him to sleep across the back seat, with room to store other gear they'd need so they could camp out in nice weather.

"You'll like camping out," Daddy said. "Seeing the stars every night. Listening to the crickets. Making memories."

Lulu crawled around inside, patting the makeshift mattresses and examining the built-in storage. When she came out, Serena and Aunt Ruth had gone inside the house. Lulu stood next to her father with her hands on her hips and said, "When?"

"When what?" Daddy said, looking north toward the building thunderheads, puffy and pink and orange and deep gray in the dark blue sky.

"When are we leaving?" She felt like she'd grown a thousand years older in that one month while he was gone.

He looked down at her. "When does school end for the summer break?"

26
Now

WHEN THEY woke the next morning, a half inch of snow dusted everything. It had gone from Indian summer to early winter overnight. Serena said nothing as they ate their cold Pop Tarts in the dark, huddled inside their puffy coats, the snow covering the front window. It was so cold inside the Suburban that Lulu could see her breath.

Still no Daddy.

"Montana," said Deana with a dramatic sigh, when Lulu got to school and everyone was talking about the early snow.

The other girls, and boys, too, were all wearing boots. Deana's were topped with a fur ruff that matched her princess coat. Lulu's sneakers were soaked and her feet felt like blocks of ice. She stood next to the heater until the bell rang. She thought about Serena's sneakers and Serena's feet and how cold Serena must feel. She thought about what she would do about boots and wondered whether the Lutherans had any boot giveaways.

She thought about Daddy.

She thought about what she ought to do now. Almost a week, and not a word, not a peep.

Last time it had been a month, and they'd gotten through it. But last time Lulu and Serena were with Aunt Ruth, in Aunt Ruth's honest-to-goodness house in warm-hot Texas, and not in an RV park in a Suburban with coming-on-winter in Small Town, Montana. Alone. And with almost no money.

Maybe over the weekend, at the library, she could do an Internet search for her daddy. Maybe she should go to the police. . . .

But, no, not the police. She didn't trust the police. Lulu wasn't going to let them—the grown-ups in charge—separate her from Serena, which is what she knew they would do. And they'd put them each in some home somewhere—most likely, not even in this town, or together—and that home wouldn't be home because there would be people there who didn't love them or even care much except about the money that they got for fostering (or that's what Lulu knew, that's what she'd overheard from Aunt Ruth, and from kids she knew in the past, and she was pretty sure Aunt Ruth didn't want them, not at all), and if that happened Lulu might never see Serena again, and Daddy would come back to the empty Suburban in the RV park and ask, "Where? Where are you?"

Like Lulu asked to the dark night now, every night now.

So, no. Lulu was not going to let anything get between her and Serena. She just had to keep figuring out the details.

Daddy used to say, before he went off that first time, right after the whole thing started, "One day at a time, girls. One day at a time."

That's what she'd do. Take it one day at a time. One detail at a time. Checking the Internet at the library on Saturday would be okay, and that gave her a small glint of hope.

But first, she had to fake the note from Daddy so she could walk Serena home and not get Laurie in trouble.

Then, she had to find boots.

Miss Baker's voice broke through Lulu's thoughts. ". . . starting the writing team program next Monday. I'll be pairing you up with your partner."

Quiet groans rose through the classroom, and quieter whispers, as friends hoped to be paired with friends and not with "her" or "him."

At lunch, Jack plunked down across from Lulu and then didn't move, except to slowly slide his milk onto her tray, staring straight at her the whole time. "That was awesome, that thing yesterday," he said at last.

That thing where he danced and she sang and they had been somewhere else entirely and she'd been someone else entirely, even for those few minutes. That magical thing they'd made together. That magical thing they were going to try and make happen again, the next afternoon, at the tryouts.

Lulu nodded, and because she was pulled for that moment out of thinking about the other stuff, she smiled. Then the other stuff crowded back in. "I need a favor." Detail one.

Jack, his mouth filled with cornbread, nodded.

"I need you to help me write a note."

He wiped his face with the back of his hand. "Sure. No problem."

Lulu slid the paper across the table. It was blank white, and she held a black pen. "I'll dictate, okay?"

He squinted a second, then shrugged. "Okay."

"'To Whom It May Concern.'"

Jack leaned over and began to write.

"Can you make it look like grown-up handwriting?" Lulu asked.

"Um, what's grown-up handwriting?"

"You know, neat and all."

He watched her.

"'Please let Lulu Johnson bring her sister Serena home from after-school.'"

Jack wrote, then sat back. "Um . . ."

"'Sincerely, John Johnson.'"

Jack put down the pen. "Wait. I'm writing a note from your dad?"

Lulu pushed what was left of her lunch around the plate,

suddenly not hungry. She didn't look up when she said, "Is that a problem?"

There was a long silence. Then Jack bent over and finished the note, and pushed it and the pen back to her.

"Is your dad okay?" he asked in a voice so quiet and full of concern that Lulu had to fight hard to keep those tears locked up.

Finally she nodded. "Just can't write," she said, because she couldn't say more.

"Oh! Golly. Gosh, you know, my mom teaches adults to read and write. You know, the ones who can't. She's really good at it." Jack was talking so fast, like he was filling up an empty bucket with words.

That wasn't what Lulu had meant, but it was a relief, and she realized, a great way out. Yes! If her daddy couldn't read and write, of course he couldn't write a note! She looked up at Jack and nodded. "Thanks. I'll tell him."

When I see him.

I'll tell him. Lulu looked down again.

I'll tell him. Lulu clenched her fist.

I'll tell him. Lulu would not cry.

She reached across the table to take the note and the pen, and forced herself to smile at Jack as she forced her other feelings deep, deep down inside.

27

Before

LULU HAD already started leaving things behind long before she pulled herself up into the Suburban to head north, and not just the stuff in her life.

When Mama got sick, Lulu had the feeling that some of her friends thought it might be contagious and that Lulu might be a carrier. Or maybe they thought that it was too darn hard to talk to Lulu who had a sick mama and what was the right thing to say, anyhow? Her friends began to avoid her, give her these weird looks, and she was too busy to do anything about it.

When Mama was gone Lulu felt like everything was done, and she just didn't have the strength to try.

The worst was when they had the last big yard sale and Lulu put out her favorite chair, the one her mama had rocked her in and then rocked Serena in when they were babies, the one with the seat cushion that Mama had made out of a patch-work of their baby clothes. Lulu's best friend's mama bought that chair for all of twenty dollars, "because it'll need a little fixing up with those scratches and such."

How could she ever go into Olivia's house again, with that chair in Olivia's bedroom, with that seat cushion on Lulu's chair? Or worse, with the seat cushion cast aside, replaced by some floral fabric that matched Olivia's floral wallpaper?

From that moment on, Lulu crumpled up inside and closed everything away, closed all the doors and windows, all the closets and curtains. She locked the entry and threw away the key.

When Daddy pulled out of Aunt Ruth's driveway before dawn on that June morning, Lulu didn't look back.

28
Now

"Lulu," Miss Baker said on Thursday, "please stop by my desk on your way out."

Lulu heard the snarky whispered words from behind her. Deana shoved Lulu's shoulder slightly as she passed.

"You too, Deana," said Miss Baker.

At that, the whole world stopped turning.

Everyone froze for an instant, and then there was a mad dash for the door to the classroom as the rest of the class except Lulu and Deana left. No one wanted to be caught in the middle.

Deana froze just inside the doorway, her hand on the jamb.

Lulu, who was already waiting at Miss Baker's desk, concentrated on a series of scratches in the wood desktop, scratches that ran in circles, in loops, like a group of acrobats soaring in two dimensions.

"Girls, I want you to be partners in the writing team program for the next two weeks. Deana, you know the ropes, so I hope you'll help guide Lulu."

"Now, Miss Baker," Deana said, in a voice full of pain. "You are aware that I have allergies."

Silence. The acrobats whirled and twirled.

"And?" said Miss Baker.

"Well, I mean," Deana drawled. Lulu thought she could be from Texas, the way she stretched her words thin and long like taffy. "The, you know. The odors." She fanned her face.

"I'm sorry?" said Miss Baker.

Deana heaved an Academy Award–worthy sigh. "Miss Baker. I mean, does she have any other clothes?"

Silence. Miss Baker pursed her lips. Then she said softly, "Deana, I think you're better than that."

Deana said, "Miss Baker." But she sounded weird, her voice pinched now, the taffy hard.

The acrobats flew into the air and turned turned turned, with circles like pinwheels. Lulu swallowed so hard she was sure Deana could hear it.

"You and Lulu will be partners. Starting Monday. No excuses." Miss Baker's voice was tight, and when Lulu glanced up, she was surprised to see a smile on her teacher's face. "Thank you, Deana."

Deana left, shutting the door hard behind.

Lulu traced the circles on the desktop with her finger now. Then she turned to leave.

"Lulu. Stay a sec."

Lulu sucked in air.

"You're a talented writer. You've shown that in just these few weeks."

Lulu glanced up quick, then back down at the acrobats. Miss Baker had just told her she was a talented writer. What did that mean?

"Deana is . . . challenged with writing. But she has other skills, like her imagination, that she hides because she wants to be popular. She can help you make your great writing even better, and you can help her channel her ideas into great writing. Now, I know she can be difficult, but I think if the two of you work together, you can bring out each other's strengths. Can you help Deana with that, Lulu?"

Could she? Could she help someone else, when Lulu felt like she was drowning? Could she help someone else when her world was crashing around her like those acrobats that were falling to earth without a net? Could she help anyone but herself and Serena and, and . . .

Step up. Do what needed doing. Yes, she could.

"Okay."

Miss Baker reached out and patted Lulu's hand. "Okay. See you tomorrow."

29
Way Before

SHE LOOKED so small. Shrunken.

"Mama?" Lulu whispered.

Lulu was afraid to touch her. Afraid she would break her own mama with her touch.

Lulu's mama had been a superhero.

Super librarian.

Super mom.

Super wife.

Super strong.

Riding a bike like she rode in the Tour de France. Moving furniture like she performed in the WWF. Singing in the church choir—not just like an angel—like she was an archangel, with a voice to reach the throne of heaven.

And then.

The doctors were in and out, in and out, but they didn't seem to be doing much, because maybe they couldn't. There were lots of tubes and liquids and nurses and beeps and machines and this stuff, it was all happening over and over, lots of terrible medical things, ever since that day when Lulu's mama had thrown her hand to her chest and said, "Oh!"

Just that.

"Oh!"

And then, boom.

The only other thing Lulu knew was that her daddy was watching the doctors and asking questions and trying to keep track, and every night, he looked at papers in a stack on the table underneath the yellow globe light, a stack that grew very tall, but mostly he was trying to breathe, just breathe, as Lulu's mama was breathing less and less, and Lulu and Serena were needing more and more, and everyone else around them seemed to need more, too, and there just wasn't any more to give.

Lulu was alone in the darkened hospital room with her mama. Daddy had taken Serena to the bathroom and Aunt Ruth had gone to call the nurse because the beeping had gone funny. Lulu leaned over her mother, so tiny now, so fragile. "Mama?" she whispered.

In that moment Lulu suddenly couldn't breathe right, like her breath was stuck inside her chest.

Lulu's mama opened her eyes, looked straight at Lulu, and said, her first word in days, "Lulu." Then her eyes grew wide and she looked far past Lulu, far far away. She whispered, sounding amazed, "Look at all those wings."

30
Now

LAURIE SQUINTED as she read the note. She looked up at Lulu, then back at the paper in her hand. "Okay," she said, not sounding like it was okay at all. Sounding like she could tell that the letter was a fake. Lulu had been so nervous about its fakeness that she didn't give it to Laurie yesterday. "At least you finally remembered to bring a note." Laurie turned away and turned back again. "But I'd really like to speak with your father as soon as he's better. Okay?"

Lulu nodded. As soon as he was better.

"Um," Lulu said, "there's another thing. I'll be a little late tomorrow."

"Like how late?" Laurie sounded impatient.

"Maybe closer to five thirty?"

"We're supposed to close at five."

"I know," Lulu said. "But there's something I really want to do."

Laurie sighed. "No later than five thirty. I've got things to do, too, you know. I don't live here. Plus, they lock up the school."

"Okay. I know. Thank you. Thank you so much. I'll be here."

Laurie moved away, muttering.

Lulu sat down next to Serena, who was folding paper again. She pushed her homework aside and began folding, too.

"What're you making?" Serena asked in an unusually soft voice.

"A paper crane," Lulu said.

"I wish you could make a pair of boots."

Lulu bent down and touched Serena's sneakers. They were still damp. "I'll figure something out," Lulu said. "The snow's melted, at least." She tried to sound happy.

It had melted but it was still cold outside, and wet, and even Lulu's feet still felt soggy. What would she do tomorrow if their shoes didn't dry?

By the time they left the after-school, Lulu had made nineteen paper cranes. Her fingers were achy. She tucked the cranes carefully inside her backpack so they wouldn't get crushed. Only nineteen. Nine hundred and eighty-one to go.

The days were growing short now, so as they walked back to the Suburban the sky was purpling with a thin band of pink in the western horizon. Maybe that meant it would be sunny the next day. Lulu sure hoped so. Serena's hand felt cold and she realized they needed gloves as well as boots.

Daddy hadn't planned for the Montana winter, had he? Lulu wondered if he'd really known. And now she couldn't ask him because he'd gone missing.

As they passed Mrs. Rogers's trailer, the RV park manager stepped out through the door and called to Lulu.

"Where's your daddy, honey?"

Lulu, still walking, answered, "Working a late shift." She sped up her pace.

"Next week's rent is due Monday," Mrs. Rogers called.

Lulu waved her hand. Next week's rent. Twenty dollars. She only had fifteen and change.

When they'd first arrived in the RV park, Daddy had said Mrs. Rogers "looked the other way" about them living there. But without Daddy and especially without the rent Lulu couldn't trust that Mrs. Rogers would keep on looking the other way.

She didn't glance back to see if Mrs. Rogers was still watching as they made their way to the Suburban.

By the time they reached the car Serena was sniffling. Lulu bundled them both into the shower, turning the water up hot. The whole time, she thought about smelling nice instead of having "odors," so she used extra soap from her bottle, even though it was running low. When they got out of the shower,

Lulu used the hand dryer to dry their hair—which kept shutting off, of course—and then she held their sneakers under the hand dryer until Serena complained about being hungry.

Lulu heated some soup on the camp stove, and then tucked Serena into the blankets. She felt Serena's forehead. It was warm.

What would she do if Serena got sick?

Lulu spent most of the night staring at the inside roof of the Suburban, her eyes tracing the curves from the middle of the roof down to the fogged-up windows.

31

LULU, YAWNING, started the car the next morning for the first time since their daddy had disappeared. To warm it up inside. Just to be able to get dressed in warmth.

She knew she couldn't keep it running for very long because at some point during their trip Daddy had told them that it was unhealthy to sit in a running car without driving. "Fumes," he said. "They're like poison, inside a running car when the air outside is cold."

Plus, she could see that the gas tank was down to a quarter.

But, oh, boy, was it nice to have that heater running this morning, and she rested their sneakers right on top of the defroster vent. She even turned on the radio, soft, to help cheer up Serena, who was sneezing a lot. They ate their Pop Tarts to Taylor Swift. Lulu counted two Pop Tarts left from their jumbo box—she'd have to find some other breakfast at the food bank. She boiled some water and made weak coffee out of what Daddy had left. She dug out clean clothes from the duffel to go with her soapy shower smell. It was Friday, after all, and laundry day was Saturday, so she could wear something clean and not worry about having nothing to wear later.

Wait. It was Friday.

The day of the tryouts. A small tickle ran through Lulu's chest and she hummed along to "ME!" hoping to loosen her froggy vocal chords. She wanted so much to feel again the way she felt when she and Jack had practiced.

While Serena brushed her teeth, Lulu lined up the paper cranes on the Suburban's still-warm dashboard. They were a riot of color.

One thousand paper cranes for the wish to come true, as the legend said. One thousand, made within one year. Lulu didn't have a year. She and Serena needed boots, like, yesterday. She wanted her daddy to reappear, like, right now.

Nine days now. Nine days missing. Things were getting harder and harder, but she had to stand up and make it all right. So, if she believed that her wish to have him back would come true, she'd have to work fast, making all those paper cranes. Because making those cranes, which were supposed to help make her wish come true, was her only hope.

The cranes made the Suburban look festive, even from the outside as Lulu locked the car.

Their sneakers were dry now, and it hadn't snowed again. In fact, the sun was shining when they left the RV park. Lulu sped past Mrs. Rogers's trailer as fast as she could, clutching Serena's warm little hand.

With the sun and the boost she got from the coffee and the image of those bright cranes and the anticipation of the tryouts and the sudden hope that she could make her wish come true by doing something so, so simple as making paper cranes, Lulu's heart lifted. She started to hum "ME!" again, and then managed to get Serena to sing it with her, even though Serena sneezed every few minutes.

By the time Lulu reached her classroom her heart was so light it felt like one of those colorful cranes. In fact, it felt just like the rosy pink crane that Lulu had placed in the very center of the Suburban's front window.

32

THE DAY went either way too fast, or way too slowly.

The morning crawled. Lulu hadn't studied for the spelling test but she'd aced it anyway. History was all about the American Revolution, and she knew just enough to squeak through the classroom questions. Math was geometry, and she couldn't help noticing the triangles, which reminded her of the folds she made in the paper cranes.

Then suddenly it was lunch and she was sitting across from Jack, whose face was pink with excitement, the same pink as the crane. As her heart.

"So, I've had this idea," he said, breathless. "What if we both sang?" He shoved a much-crumpled sheet of paper toward her. "What if we alternated the lines, sort of like we were performing it?"

Lulu turned the paper so she could read it. Jack had detailed the lines, with a *J* beside some and an *L* beside the others.

"Wait," said Lulu. "You can dance *and* sing?"

"Well, I don't sing like you," he said, and fiddled with his mac and cheese. "I mean, I can carry a tune. But you're amazing. But if we both sang, it would be really fun."

Lulu's face went hot. She fiddled with her own mac and cheese. "Sure. That's a neat idea. But, um, I can't dance."

"Don't worry," he said. "I've got a plan. It'll be great. I promise."

After lunch, the day raced, as Lulu grew more and more nervous. She'd never auditioned for anything before. She'd never thought about auditioning for anything before. She sang in the church choir because her mama did, and nobody had asked her to audition.

She didn't know what to expect, except that when the three o'clock bell rang, it was like those paper cranes were flying around inside her stomach.

Jack had signed them up for a slot at four so they could watch some of the other auditions first. Everyone had ten minutes. Lulu sat with Jack to one side. The three teachers who were judging sat at a table right up front. Mr. Franzen, who taught English but was in charge of the drama program, went on a bit about how the auditions worked and how not to be nervous although it was okay to be nervous (a little laugh) and how there was a role for everyone to play, even if it was tech support (another little laugh), just do your best and break a leg, all of which made Lulu even more nervous.

"Why did he tell us to break a leg?" she whispered to Jack. "Who wants that?"

"It's a theater thing. You're not supposed to say good luck."

Lulu, looking down at her own legs in her jeans, thought that was the strangest thing she'd ever heard.

A high school student sat at the piano on the stage to accompany the singers. When Deana stepped forward and told the student what she was singing, Lulu looked at Jack.

"She's in every play," he whispered. "She always gets the lead role." Then he added, more softly, "Until now."

Deana had a nice voice. Lulu was surprised. Impressed, even. Deana sang "Over the Rainbow," and when she was done, her friends, sitting all the way in the back of the theater, clapped until Mr. Franzen shushed them.

Then it was their turn.

Jack told the pianist "Simple Gifts," and Lulu swallowed hard. She was supposed to sing the first lines. The pianist started with the opening chords, and . . .

Lulu botched the entry.

Jack stepped up and said, "Sorry. Can we start over? My fault."

It wasn't his fault at all. Lulu swallowed again, and Jack

looked at her and smiled and nodded. The pianist began a second time, and this time Lulu hit the first notes, but so soft she could hardly even hear herself.

Deana and her friends began to whisper-talk and laugh, and Mr. Franzen stood up. "Stop!" he commanded.

Everything and everyone went silent.

Mr. Franzen turned and faced the back rows. "If you girls can't be quiet you may leave." He turned back, and waved his hand. "Again, please." He sounded impatient, and wasn't looking at Lulu or Jack.

For the third time, the pianist began the intro, and this time Jack took the mic and began to sing at the same time Lulu did. She turned to him and, understanding, leaned into the mic and harmonized with him. Then, when the moment came in the chorus, Jack paused for her, and then she paused for him, and then they sang together again.

Some kind of magic happened, some kind of magic where it was only Lulu and Jack and the girl at the piano, and then—while he was singing—Jack made a little bow and extended his hand and twirled Lulu in a little dance—while she was singing. Lulu thought she was right inside that song, and she had never felt that much magic in her whole life. She repeated the chorus by herself and then sang the last two lines with her eyes closed, clutching the mic right to her mouth.

To turn, turn will be our delight,

Till by turning, turning, we come round right.

The song ended, and Lulu heard her voice, her own voice, rich with emotion, *we come round right,* echoing into silence— even the piano was silent, breathless.

Lulu opened her eyes; Jack was beaming.

33

Way, Way Before

LULU SANG the hymn in the back seat as her mama drove home through the twilight. Lulu loved that hymn. "Swing Low, Sweet Chariot." Her mama joined in the chorus, in harmony, and Lulu never wanted this moment to end, singing with her mama, their voices in a perfect blend.

Comin' for to carry me home.

Mama pulled over to the curb and turned to look over the seat. "C'mon up front."

Lulu sat up, not quite certain. "In the front seat?"

Mama nodded. "You're a big girl now," she said. "Plus, we're almost home."

Lulu moved into the front seat, fastening the seat belt as Mama watched, a smile on her face. "I'm going to tell you a secret," she said.

Lulu waited.

"I'm leaving my job to stay at home for a while."

"But, I thought you liked your job. I mean, being a librarian is so cool."

"Oh, I do love it. But your daddy's job is going well, and I've got a kind of surprise." She sat back in the seat, still smiling, and patted her belly.

"Mama, are you . . . ," Lulu began, breathless.

Mama nodded, smiling huge. "You're going to be a big sister to another little one. The way I see it, you're already so good with Serena . . ."

Lulu unbuckled the seat belt and moved across the seat, and threw her arms around her mama. "Is it a boy or a girl?"

Mama laughed. "No idea yet, honey." She paused, staring out the front. "You sing like an angel, Lu. I hope you keep singing always."

"I'll sing to the baby," Lulu said, and giggled, excited. "Just like I sang to Serena when she was a baby."

Mama laughed again, and then, her expression suddenly serious, said, "Seat belt."

Three months later, Lulu's mama threw her hand to her chest and said, "Oh!"

That "Oh!" was the worst sound Lulu had ever heard up to that moment. She didn't know that much worse would come.

Mama got sick and sicker from the cancer, and Lulu held tight to her hand, but Mama lost the baby anyhow, so there was no baby. Lulu sang to her mama, sitting by her bedside, trying to hold on, trying to make it all right through sheer force of will.

And then there was no Mama.

34

Before

LULU WAS sure that Aunt Ruth didn't mean to be mean. She was just tough, and old, and didn't understand.

Daddy had been gone for almost the whole month when it happened. Lulu heard the commotion at the door, and she'd already heard Aunt Ruth on the phone. Lulu could tell it wasn't their daddy returning but something maybe not good, so she told Serena to stay upstairs with the door closed while she went to check.

Standing just around the corner at the top of the stairs she heard Aunt Ruth talking loud about Lulu and Serena. When Lulu peeked through the bannister she saw a police officer and a woman in a suit with Aunt Ruth. There were words said among the three grown-ups that made Lulu cold all over. She knew enough kids in school who went through hard times. She knew exactly what they meant, those words.

"Foster."

"Abandoned."

She heard them talking about when and how. About getting the paperwork started. About what would happen. They talked about meeting Lulu and Serena right then and there, but when Aunt Ruth called up the stairs, Lulu didn't answer and the grown-ups decided to wait a day or two.

When the police officer and the woman in the suit left, Lulu knew that she'd better do something. She had to stand up, right then.

She confronted Aunt Ruth in her kitchen. Every part of Lulu's body tingled like she was touching a live wire.

"Mama will never forgive you," she said, and her voice shook.

Aunt Ruth's eyes widened and then glinted.

"Daddy will be back," Lulu said. "And Mama will never forgive you."

"Your mama's gone." Aunt Ruth turned away, rubbing her eyes.

"Don't," Lulu said, her voice hard.

"Your daddy's gone. And I don't know what to do," Aunt Ruth said.

Lulu stood in Aunt Ruth's kitchen, her feet braced wide apart, her back straight as a stick. For the first time ever, she was talking back to a grown-up. "I'm saying that you will not do that. You will not send us away," Lulu said, her voice shaking. "Daddy will be back."

Daddy did come back two days later, and he drove the Suburban north the day after school finished for summer break, and Lulu had stood up for herself and Serena when he hadn't been there.

And she would stand up again and again, yes she would.

35
Now

"THEY'LL POST the parts on Tuesday," Jack said. "Then rehearsals start Thursday."

Lulu and Jack walked out into the cold air, side by side. Lulu was still giddy. As they'd left the stage, the pianist had whispered, with a smile, "Beautiful." Lulu hadn't dared to look at the judges, especially Mr. Franzen. She didn't notice whether Deana was still there or not.

Lulu automatically started walking toward the elementary school to pick up Serena. She was floating toward her sister.

Jack stopped walking. "Um, I have to go that way." He pointed up the side street. "But, well, I can walk you home, if you want. Or we can get together tomorrow. Maybe we can practice a little more. I can show you some of the songs and dance steps in *Schoolhouse Rock*. You'll like it. Tomorrow?"

"Oh!" Lulu was suddenly cold, her feet like blocks of ice,

and she zipped up her puffy coat and tugged on her hat. It was getting dark. "No, that's okay. And you don't need to walk me home. I'm picking up my sister at after-school."

"So that's what the note was about? You picking up your sister?" he said. "I can walk you there."

"Serena. I have to take her home." Lulu paused. Home. "I'll see you Monday."

Jack's face fell. "Oh. Okay. Never mind, then. So, okay. Have a nice weekend."

He turned away and started walking fast, up the street.

"Jack!" Lulu called.

He stopped. He looked so crushed. Lulu wished . . . so many things.

"That was really amazing," she said, meaning it. "That audition."

Jack smiled, and then did a funny thing. He danced, just a few steps, then posed for a second, arms akimbo as if he was a famous actor or something. "Yeah," he said. "It was."

36

Saturday morning Lulu told Serena to sleep in. There was no question now that Serena had a cold.

"I'll get things done. You rest," Lulu said.

Serena nodded. She didn't feel too hot to the touch. Not like she had a real serious fever or anything. It was just a cold. Serena just needed rest. That's what Lulu kept saying to herself. Serena would be better off staying quiet in the Suburban than traipsing around outside with Lulu. She made sure to lock the car, and made sure to slip carefully past Mrs. Rogers's trailer.

Lulu went to the food bank first, as always. She stocked up on chicken noodle soup, the remedy her mama had believed would cure almost anything. She could stock up on more fresh food, too, since it was colder now and the car wouldn't get so hot. And though they didn't have Pop Tarts at the food bank, they did have cereal bars, which were almost as good.

As she was checking out of the food bank, one of the workers stopped her. She'd seen him there lots of Saturdays. She had the feeling he knew what it was like to be hungry. He said, "Where's your daddy, hon?"

"He's working extra," she said, the now familiar lie.

"You kids okay?" He seemed nice, this guy, but Lulu gripped the handles on the shopping cart hard. After what had happened at the oil field she was extra wary.

"We're good," she said, and sped out of there, right back to the Suburban.

There was the note waiting for her, under the windshield wiper, about next week's rent due, twenty dollars. Monday. With a smiley face.

Lulu sat in the front seat and counted the money again. When she finished the laundry, she'd have a little over ten dollars left. She could skip doing the laundry, but that still wouldn't leave her with enough to pay the RV park. Plus, she wouldn't skip the laundry because she didn't want to give Deana any reason to wrinkle her nose.

Lulu made sure that Serena was still okay by herself—she was still sleeping, and Lulu figured that was good for her—and she checked that the stack of colored paper Laurie had given her was in her backpack, and headed for the laundromat, carrying the laundry in a pillowcase.

She stopped at the library on the way. Ms. M was at the

children's desk, stacking books on the rolling cart. "Lulu! It's nice to see you. Have you given any thought to that library corner at the laundromat? What books we could put there?"

"Picture books," Lulu said. "There are always lots of little kids there with nothing to do."

"Great! We're on the same page." Ms. M smiled. "I was thinking of making it kind of like a little free library. You know, with books there on the honor system. Do you think that would work?"

Lulu nodded. "'Cause even if they take them home, that's okay, right? 'Cause maybe they don't have any books at home."

Ms. M leaned over the desk, and said solemnly, "Exactly." She reached behind her and lifted a stack of picture books onto the desk. "I set these aside last week. What do you think of my choices?"

Lulu fingered the books, one after the other, nodding. Lots of books about lots of different kids. Kids who looked like Lulu and kids who didn't. Books about kindness and books about sharing. Books about animals and books about plants. Lulu nodded again.

Ms. M went on, "Okay, then. I'll go there with you now. I've got something in my car that my husband made for me, just for this. I'll bring you back here when you finish your laundry. Mrs. Everts will cover for me." She paused. "Or I can drop you off at your house, if you want."

"No, that's okay," Lulu said fast. "I like to walk."

Being in someone else's car felt weird, especially since it was also a Suburban. But the trunk of Ms. M's car was full with something made out of wood instead of bedding, and Ms. M's car was super clean and shiny. Lulu sat in the second seat clutching the pillowcase, the stack of picture books on the cushiony seat next to her, and her backpack at her feet.

It took two minutes to get to the laundromat by car. Lulu helped Ms. M carry the wood pieces inside to the far empty corner of the big room and Ms. M started putting the pieces together with tools, like a giant wooden puzzle. The owner of the laundromat was there, smiling, lending a hand. The pieces turned out to be a set of shelves with a countertop and a painted sign saying PUBLIC LIBRARY! HELP YOURSELF TO A BOOK! NO NEED FOR A LIBRARY CARD! and instructions for how it would work. Ms. M had also brought beanbag chairs. Lulu stacked the books neatly on the shelves before she started her laundry.

Ms. M moved around the laundromat, talking to the moms and kids, and pretty soon there were four or five little ones sprawled across the beanbags, reading books and pointing out the stuff in the pictures.

It was neat that Ms. M's husband made those shelves. Lulu's daddy could have made something like that. The thought made Lulu's heart zing painfully and she wondered again where, where, where he could be, leaving as he did, leaving her and Serena and his own tools and his job. She hadn't had time at the library to search the Internet for him, like she'd planned, and she didn't want Ms. M to know what she was doing. She just wanted him to come back, and now also because she wanted to stop worrying about feeling so helpless about not knowing where to begin to look.

Was it just like the last time, when he'd come back with the Suburban? Was it like last time, when he'd left because he was broken and came back when he'd put himself together, like these shelves? Was he going to come back to Lulu and Serena this time with something even bigger than the Suburban, and with his heart fully mended?

But why hadn't he said anything before going? Why, in this strange town, had he up and disappeared without a word? Had he gotten lost? She'd heard about people who lost their memories after an accident. Is that what had happened to him? Or was it something worse that Lulu still couldn't bear to imagine?

Last time he'd left them with Aunt Ruth. This time he'd left them alone.

Lulu's fear and sadness, once again, turned sharply, abruptly, unexpectedly toward anger. Lulu was tired of worrying. Tired of taking care of herself and Serena all by herself. Sure, she'd stepped up. But she wanted to be like the little kids who were laughing in this sudden new library corner, rolling around on the beanbags, their moms gossiping over T-shirts and jeans and matching socks, looking like they'd landed in a tub of butter with their kids reading and having fun.

Lulu was not having fun.

Not at all.

This was so unfair.

Lulu jammed the two quarters into the dryer coin tray and shoved the tray into the slot, listening to the quarters clink into place and away. The machine was sucking up two of her last quarters. When Lulu turned around she saw that Ms. M was watching her, even while Ms. M was still sitting with the little ones, reading them book after book.

Lulu sat across the room in the opposite corner and began furiously folding paper cranes.

37

SERENA SLEPT much of the weekend. Lulu was able to give her some soup, and by Monday Lulu thought she was well enough to go back to school.

"You should go to the school nurse only if you feel really bad," Lulu said. "Because the school nurse will want to call Daddy, and then what?" Lulu chewed her lip. "We don't want the school nurse to know that Daddy's not here, do we? Or that we've been living in the Suburban alone, right?"

Serena shuffled along, clutching Lulu's hand.

"I can't leave you in the Suburban all alone all day," Lulu said. "And if we don't show up to school someone might ask questions."

"And then what?" Serena murmured. Lulu thought Serena might be thinking that if someone came asking questions, that would be a good thing. But Lulu knew otherwise.

Yellow and orange leaves pinwheeled down around them, blowing into the gutter.

"It's just a cold, Reenie. You'll be okay."

Lulu had taken the ten dollars to Mrs. Rogers on Sunday afternoon, and told her that "the rest was coming." Mrs. Rogers squinted and asked again, "Where's your daddy?" And Lulu had said again, "Working extra. Comes in late at night and leaves real early in the morning." Mrs. Rogers had started in on not being a charity, and that she wasn't at all sure about any of this since she hadn't seen Lulu's daddy in days, and the whole time Mrs. Rogers talked Lulu was backing away, off the trailer's porch and up the dirt road. Mrs. Rogers was following and talking louder and louder and the only reason Lulu got away was that Mrs. Rogers was wearing hair curlers and must not have wanted everyone to see her like that, so she eventually gave up and went back to her trailer muttering.

"It's just a cold," Lulu said again to her sister.

Serena coughed, as if to make a point.

"I'll see you in after-school, okay?" Lulu stood at the door of the elementary and watched her sister plod away heavy-footed. Serena's hair hung down her back and over her Hello Kitty pack in messy strings.

The whole entire weekend Lulu had made paper cranes. She made paper cranes until she ran out of paper. Then she counted them up and found that she'd made one hundred and forty-seven. They were piled on the dash of the Suburban all the way up the window to the top, and then some.

It was a lot of paper cranes but it wasn't even close to one thousand.

And what about her wish, the one for which she was making all those paper cranes?

She wished that Daddy would come back. That was her first and most pressing wish.

But now she also wished that Serena would be okay. And she wished that she had money for boots for both of them. And money for laundry and the car and other things. And even money to buy chocolate chip cookies, which they didn't have at the food pantry, where the food was good but not great.

Then there was the biggest wish of all, the dream wish. The one about not living in the Suburban any longer. About having a house to live in again, like they'd had once upon a time.

She also wished, since very recently, that she would get a part in the school play, because that was the one place in Lulu's life right now where all the rest of this wishing-ness disappeared.

Oh, how Lulu wished. A house. A home, with Daddy there. With Serena fine. With money. And a way for Lulu to sing to her heart's content.

Happiness. A real life. Hope.

Lulu figured that a thousand paper cranes wouldn't even come close to making all that come true. She'd need ten thousand.

Maybe a million.

A million paper cranes.

For all her million wishes.

38

MISS BAKER briefly explained the writing partnerships and then had each member of the pair sit next to the other. Because of space and the fact that they had to talk, some pairs stayed in the classroom, and some were sent to the library.

Deana and Lulu were sent to the library.

They sat at a library table opposite one another. Deana had been unusually quiet already this morning, and she still wasn't saying anything. They sat for a few minutes, and then Deana, looking down at the table and shuffling her book and pencil, said, "You're really good."

Lulu said, "Um . . ."

"Singing. You're a really good singer."

"Oh! Thanks! You are, too! I mean, really."

Deana tap-tap-tapped her pencil on the desk, fast then faster. "Anyhoo."

"Any what?"

"Anyhoo. Like, you know, anyways."

"Oh." Lulu had never heard of "*anyhoo*." She thought it must be a Montana thing. "We're supposed to write, I guess."

"So I have an idea, because we're supposed to write something like a short story first, right?"

Lulu nodded.

"So what about if these kids go to the moon?"

Lulu raised her eyebrows and then opened her notebook. "Okay . . ."

And before Lulu knew what was happening, Deana was spouting this elaborate science fiction story about kids on the moon, and Lulu was trying to write down as much as she could, and the two of them were talking, actually talking, and suddenly out of nowhere they were laughing—actually laughing—and then before she knew it, the bell rang. They were still talking excitedly about the idea and the story until they were halfway back to the classroom and then Deana suddenly went back to being quiet.

"So . . . ," Lulu said.

"So, great. Maybe you could write it up. Because I'm not a great writer, I'll admit. Like, my grammar stinks."

"Sure," said Lulu. "Okay."

Deana squared her shoulders and marched into the classroom without looking at Lulu, as if the past hour had never happened.

Lulu stood on the threshold of the classroom for a minute before she made her way to her desk and to the rest of the school day, confused. No, bewildered. What had happened with Deana?

At lunch she was still bewildered, but Jack was all but bouncing with excitement.

"I think we've got a real shot."

"At?" she said.

"At being the leads. You were awesome." He took a huge bite of his sandwich and then said, "How was your weekend?" Though because his mouth was so stuffed with sandwich it sort of came out, "Ow us or eekend?"

"Um, okay," Lulu said, not meeting his eyes. Then, wanting to say something, said, "I'm helping the public librarian set up a little free library in the laundromat."

Jack bounced higher. "Ms. Maurene? She's my next-door neighbor. She's great."

A tickle of worry crept into Lulu. "Really?" she said. But so close, too close, Jack and Ms. M living right next door to each other. What if they talked about Lulu? Figured out what was happening to Lulu? Figured out that her daddy had gone missing? Could Lulu trust any adult, even Ms. M? No. No, she could not. And she couldn't bear it if Jack found out. "Well, I don't really know her well or anything like that."

"Maybe I could help with the library. In the laundromat, you said? Don't know where that is but I might be able to help."

Lulu stiffened, then stood up. "Got to go to science." Then, seeing Jack's expression, added, "Tomorrow we'll know, right?"

"Right! Tomorrow afternoon! But I'm betting already."

She smiled, lips tight.

39

LULU HADN'T been able to make any paper cranes for the whole afternoon and night, though she got a lot more paper when Laurie wasn't looking. Between trying to quietly take care of Serena without making a fuss or raising suspicions—Serena, who was really coughing in after-school, and still not talking much to Lulu or anyone else—and then starting the science fiction story that she and Deana had to work on, and then doing her other homework, and then taking a shower and helping Serena take a shower even though Serena complained the whole time, and then making dinner for the two of them (in the dark because now it was completely dark by the time they finished their showers), Lulu was done in.

Once again she lay in their makeshift bed in the Suburban, under all their blankets plus Daddy's, after Serena fell asleep and was snoring to beat the band. Lulu stared up at the inside roof. The roof of their teeny-tiny cold home.

Only one hundred forty-seven paper cranes. That left . . . eight hundred fifty-three to go. Or more, with all these wishes.

Lulu pressed the heels of her hands into her eyes. How much longer? How much more?

Where was he?

She tried to think about the school play and singing. She dug out her earphones and her old iPod—the one she had held on to through thick and thin—and discovered that the iPod was dead. She had no way to charge it without turning on the Suburban.

So she just began to hum, as soft as she could.

To bow and to bend we shan't be ashamed,

To turn, turn will be our delight,

Till by turning, turning we come round right.

40

"It's pretty good," Deana said, after a long silence. "Yeah." Then, "So what if, here, the kids could . . ."

Deana was off again into another long "what-if this, what-if that" on their story, and all Lulu could think as she took notes was that Miss Baker was right, Deana had a great imagination, but Lulu was so so tired and she wasn't sure she could keep it all straight. She just wrote. Blah, blah, blah wrote. Because she was really tired.

It had gotten cold again overnight. No snow, and still dry, but the walk to school with Serena coughing and the cold pavement reminded Lulu about the need for boots. About that wish.

Reminded Lulu about everything, and everything now felt like an enormous weight, like the gray puffy clouds above that were full of something ominous and it was coming down to rest on Lulu's shoulders.

What the gray puffy clouds were actually full of was snow.

It started up around lunchtime, a feathery white snowfall. It would have been pretty if Lulu had been able to enjoy it. "Early snow," said Jack. "You've got to find some boots. There's a really good shoe store on Main. Get your dad to take you there when he gets better."

Lulu nodded, staring at her rice and beans.

Jack began bouncing again. "So, if we get parts, rehearsals will start Thursday. You have the permission slip?"

"What permission slip?" Lulu asked, her chest tightening.

"Your dad'll have to sign off that you can stay late and come in some Saturdays, and that parents are asked to volunteer some. You didn't get a slip?"

Lulu remembered then that Mr. Franzen had given her a piece of paper at the beginning of the audition, but she hadn't fished it out of her backpack since.

Jack watched her carefully. Then he said, so quietly it was a whisper, "If you need me to sign it, I will. But . . ." He paused.

She waited, meeting his eyes.

"It's a lot more serious than the other one. Because I could get in trouble. You know, like, for real," he finished. He chewed his lip. "Is everything okay at home?"

Oh, how Lulu wanted to open up. Oh, how she wanted to tell. She wanted to shift the burden off her shoulders, for once, even just a little. She wanted to spill everything, right there, in the lunchroom, have Jack tell her it would be all right, have him listen, nodding, sympathetic, and offer advice and possibly help her. . . .

But Lulu knew what would happen.

First, she wouldn't be able to open up without really opening up, like with tears and stuff, and that just wasn't possible, especially in the lunchroom—plus, tears.

Second, her whole world would fall apart. Jack would probably have to tell a grown-up. He'd feel obligated to tell. They'd take her away, they'd take Serena away, and who knew if they'd ever let them be together again.

Third, what could Jack do to help? He was just a kid. Just like her. What would he do that was any different, unless it got Lulu into trouble?

And fourth, would Jack look at her the way her old Texas friends did when Mama died?

Plus, the play. The possibility of that little bit of happiness in her life.

All that would happen if Lulu opened up now to Jack was that she and Serena would be shipped off to some stranger's house, probably apart, probably somewhere else away from this school and the play, and that would end every hope Lulu had of making her dreams come true.

So she lied. "Everything's fine. Just that Daddy's been sick, and of course, he can't write real well." Lulu tried to make her voice sound normal. It was sort of like singing, she realized. Like acting. She was learning how to act. She could get better at this business. She sat straighter. "Just this once?" she said, brightly.

He nodded, sighing. "Okay. Anyway, let's meet up right after school, and we can find out together about our parts." He didn't sound so excited now.

Lulu wasn't so excited now, either, as she thought about the trouble she was making for Jack, and maybe even for Serena if she and Jack got parts and had to rehearse and might have to stay late and even on Saturdays. What would Laurie say then?

But Lulu and Jack met up by the bulletin board, and they found out the good news, and he was excited again, because Lulu and Jack were both major leads in the play, and for once Deana was in a secondary role, but also was Lulu's understudy.

The hallway was filled with kids who were jumping and yelling and some who were disappointed and quiet, and Lulu saw that Deana was one of the quiet ones, but she wasn't nasty or anything, and after she left with her bevy of friends Lulu felt free to be excited, too, and yell happy yells and jump around with Jack.

Turning, turning, turning, until it turned out right.

She was happy for the first time in thirteen days, for those few minutes, those few minutes of joy.

41

THE NEXT two days flew, mainly because of the snow. It snowed about three inches Tuesday, which everyone said was weird for so early in the fall. It would get warm again, everyone said, though it didn't feel like it would get warm to Lulu. Maybe because of the snow, but Mrs. Rogers didn't seem to be out and about, which was a relief as Lulu dragged Serena as fast as possible past her trailer. Lulu decided there were some good things about Montana weather.

Lulu and Serena stayed in after-school on Tuesday for as long as they could, to keep as warm as they could before going back to the cold Suburban in the dusky dark. Lulu couldn't cook outside because of the snow so they had to eat cold food, and they tucked in after eating and went to sleep.

Eventually, for Lulu.

Sleep, when it comes, does make the time go by faster.

On Wednesday, Lulu felt their sneakers before putting them on. They were almost dry, but almost-dry sneakers are nearly as bad as wet sneakers in the cold. Serena's cough had become persistent, and Laurie had said that if it wasn't gone by the weekend, Serena couldn't come to after-school until it was gone.

The only good thing about the coming weekend was that the next Monday was a holiday so Lulu could keep Serena tucked in for three whole days, by which time Lulu was sure her sister would be fine.

Now that almost two weeks had gone by since Daddy had left, Lulu felt like she was counting down. Last time he'd been gone a month. She'd begun to hope that maybe this time was like last time. At the end of the month maybe Daddy would, magically, reappear.

Just like last time. And then everything would be fine. Serena would be fine. Lulu would be fine. Daddy would be proud of how she'd done, how she'd stepped up.

Wednesday morning Deana was very quiet as they started their writing session. Lulu wrote, and asked questions, and Deana gave her one-word answers.

When they got back to the classroom, Deana returned to her friends and one of them said in a loud voice, "*So* sorry you have to work with Miss Stinky, Dee. When do you suppose she last took a shower?"

And Deana answered, "I know, right?" although she didn't sound really enthusiastic.

When she picked up Serena Wednesday afternoon, Lulu told Laurie she'd be late again on Thursday, maybe not there until five thirty, and Laurie frowned. "You're in the what?"

"The school play. I've got a lead part." She was both a little bit worried and more than a little bit thrilled as she said it. Lead part.

Laurie threw her hands in the air. "Your dad needs to think about making some other arrangements for your sister," she said. "I've been in plays and the rehearsals can go late. We aren't supposed to be responsible past five o'clock."

Lulu nodded and worried. The play was the best thing in her life now, really the only good thing. She had to make it work. She had to.

Wednesday night, when they got back to the Suburban, there was another note about the remaining rent tucked under the windshield wiper. This time there was no smiley face. Lulu took a shower even though it was freezing when she ran in the darkness from the shower house to the Suburban. She only made eight paper cranes before her fingers began to hurt, and then she lay awake for what seemed like forever.

By Thursday morning the snow was mostly gone, as predicted, but Serena's cough wasn't any better. Another worry.

At lunch Jack signed her permission slip and didn't say anything to Lulu about it when he slid it across the table back to her.

• • •

Play rehearsal was so much fun. Within a few minutes of rehearsing, Lulu forgot about permission slips and almost everything else. Every time she figured out a new song, learned some new dance moves, learned a new line, learned stuff about being on stage, saw how the play would go, Lulu felt like she'd disappeared inside a different world, even just for an instant. Mr. Franzen complimented her acting, too.

"Just slip right inside that character, Lulu," he said.

When Lulu did slip inside her character, as if she was slipping into a new and completely different set of clothes, she felt the outer world slide away, and she felt so light and free she was almost floating. Acting was as wonderful as singing, Lulu decided.

Mr. Franzen said, with a big smile, "That's it. Great job."

Not until she checked the clock and saw that she had five minutes to pick up Serena did she worry again.

Lulu ran all the way, but she was still five minutes late.

Laurie was outside the elementary school with Serena, her coat and hat on, backpack over her back, arms folded over her chest.

"This cannot go on," Laurie said, her voice dark. "If you're late again, or your dad doesn't show up, there will be consequences." Laurie turned on her heel and headed up the street, going home.

Lulu clutched Serena's hand tight, rubbing it with her free

hand to warm it up. "One more day, Reenie, and then we'll have a long weekend to rest up. You'll be as fit as a fiddle by Tuesday."

Serena gazed at Lulu with liquid dark eyes, then coughed and coughed, her whole small body shuddering.

42

Way Before

LULU LEANED against her mama's shoulder. The baby had been a boy. She should have a little brother except he was too too little, and Mama was too too sick, and because of Mama's sickness the baby was lost. They named him Robert, and said good-bye, just Mama and Daddy and Lulu in the hospital where it happened because everyone thought Serena was also too little, too little to really understand what had happened since Robert had really never been alive-alive. Nobody had even told Serena about the baby because Mama had become sick before Robert was very big anyway and why make things harder for Serena?

"You can take care of Serena, Lulu. You will, won't you?"

"Of course, Mama," Lulu said. She was speaking into her mama's neck. They were home and Mama was in her own bed, and Lulu was lying next to her. At least for a time now, since

Robert, Mama was home, but only for now because Mama's treatments would go on and on. Lulu said, "I'll take care of Reenie until you get better."

"That's right," Mama said. "Just until I get better." She sighed and said, "Your aunt Ruth isn't great with little ones." Then, unexpectedly, she started to laugh.

Lulu's head bounced as Mama laughed, and Mama's laughter was so rare right now that Lulu sat up and started to laugh, too. They both knew Aunt Ruth was, as Mama liked to say pretty often, "a tough old nut." But she was the only relative they had, and she lived right down the street, so she'd done a lot of babysitting for Lulu and Serena.

Still.

"She's a tough old nut," Lulu said, and her mama laughed harder, which made Lulu's heart sing, then Mama placed her hand on her chest and inhaled sharp and settled down. Lulu didn't want to make her laugh again.

"That's enough, now," Mama said. "I'm going to take a nap." And she closed her eyes.

"I'll take care of Reenie, Mama, until you're all better," Lulu whispered. "You don't have to worry."

And Lulu had taken care, hadn't she, even after. Standing up to her tough old nut Aunt Ruth when standing up was needed.

43
Now

HALFWAY THROUGH Friday rehearsal, Lulu lost all track of time.

She and Jack were rehearsing a short scene where the characters meet for the first time and show one another their instruments. Lulu had to pretend to play the electric guitar, so Mr. Franzen showed her a few tricks to make it look real, and when she got the hang of it she threw herself into the scene.

Just like before, the whole world slipped away and it was just Lulu and Jack, and they sang and pretended to play their instruments (his was a horn). Lulu loved the music and loved how her voice felt and sounded, and loved the way she and Jack played off one another, and loved the "Okay! That was great, you two!" from Mr. Franzen, and loved loved *loved* the applause from the kids who were waiting for their turns.

Yes, acting was the best thing that had happened to Lulu in a long long while.

By the time they'd run through it a bunch, and Mr. Franzen wanted to move on to some of the other actors, it was almost six.

"Oh, my gosh," Lulu said. "I've got to go!" She snapped up her puffy coat, grabbed her backpack, and flew to the back of the gym.

"Okay," Jack called after her as she ran. "See you Tues—"

The gym door slammed behind her.

She ran all the way to the elementary, her coat unzipped, the wind snapping her hair across her face.

When she got there, there was no Laurie. No Serena. No anybody.

Lulu ran from door to door all the way around the school, but every door was locked. Even the night watchman didn't make an appearance. Lulu ran around to the front of the school again, and there, way up the street, her back to Lulu, was Laurie, walking away fast, walking toward her own home.

Alone. In a serious hurry.

"Laurie!" Lulu cried. "Laurie!"

Laurie turned, waiting, and even from this distance Lulu could see that Laurie's face was dark and her mouth was working.

When Lulu caught up with her, panting hard, Laurie said, "I told you. I told you there would be consequences. I told you."

"Where's Serena?" Lulu said, her voice trembling. "Where?"

"I know something's not right. Your dad hasn't been around. I don't know where you live, but something's not right. Your sister's sick and needs a doctor."

"Where?"

"I'm responsible," Laurie said, and tears formed in her eyes, her cheeks two spots of red. "I couldn't keep playing this game you've got going. Which I don't know what it's about. I just know you've been lying."

Lulu was frozen, rigid, sick. She would throw up right there.

"Look, Lulu. If you need help, I can find you help. But hiding whatever is going on, it's not the way to handle it, not when your sister needs medical attention. Not when you don't show up."

The words rang in Lulu's brain like a bell. "Where?" Lulu whispered.

"I called social services. They came and picked her up."

Lulu took a step away. "No," she said. "No, no, no, no." She really would throw up.

"They said they were taking her to the doctor. She has a fever, Lulu. She was upset when you didn't show up. She was upset about the whole thing. She was . . ." Laurie sniffed as tears rolled down her red cheeks.

"Of course she's upset," Lulu shouted, anger, fear, and horror all bundled together. "She needs to be with me. She's supposed to be with me!"

Laurie took a step toward Lulu. Lulu took a step back. "I want to help," Laurie said, sounding like her heart would break.

Lulu shook her head violently. "You don't understand. You don't. You didn't help. You made everything worse!" Then she turned and ran, ran for the Suburban.

Laurie called out, her voice fading as Lulu ran.

Social services. Sent to social services. Her Serena. Her sister. How would Lulu find Serena?

Lulu had not shown up. She had not stood up or stepped in and now Serena was gone.

"No, no, no," was the only solid thing in Lulu's brain all the way back to the RV park.

44

WHEN LULU turned the corner right before the RV park, what she saw made her skid to a stop and slide fast behind the nearest big cottonwood tree.

There was Mrs. Rogers, gesticulating wildly, her hair flying about like it had just exploded out of those curlers. There was a police car, and a policeman and police lady, side by side, taking notes and listening. There was a man Lulu recognized as the man from her daddy's job site, Hank, the construction boss who had given her Daddy's tool bag. And there was the Suburban, not where it should be, not parked in the back, in the trees, but hinged up on a hook, like a fish on a line, like the fish Daddy had caught and then released because Serena had begged him to. The Suburban was held up by the tow truck whose lights blinked red, red, and went around and around while the tow truck driver worked to secure the Suburban in place.

The tow truck driver was not going to release the Suburban. He was going to have it for supper, as if it was a not-released fish.

The front window of the Suburban was filled with the colorful paper cranes but now they were sliding, one by one and then all at once as the tow truck driver hitched the car up and up; the cranes slid off the dash and into the darkness within. Lulu's paper cranes.

Now the number of "noes" that filled Lulu's brain was countless. It might have been millions of "noes."

Then, without warning, Lulu couldn't breathe. She really couldn't breathe. She turned her back against the cottonwood tree and tried to suck in air but it was as if all the air in the world had been pulled away into the stratosphere, as if oxygen didn't exist, as if she was an alien or on another planet that didn't have oxygen in its atmosphere. Lulu closed her eyes and kept trying to breathe, but it only came faster and faster, shallow breaths, which only made things worse.

Her heart pounded in her ears, and a darkness filled her brain, pushing out the "noes" and everything else, and the darkness said, "You're dying."

This had happened to Lulu once before, in the hospital, when she hadn't been able to breathe, when Lulu's breath got stuck, and then when it stopped altogether not long after her mama had said those words in the beeping darkness, not long after when Lulu knew her mama was gone.

Look at all those wings.

If Lulu died now, she'd never find Serena. She'd never find her daddy. She'd never wear a pair of boots or act as a character onstage or ever sing again. She'd never see Jack again or Ms. M and she wouldn't finish her story with Deana. She'd never live in a real house again.

Lulu clenched her fists and tried really really hard to stop breathing fast. And that helped. She sank down to sit on the ground and breathed more slowly and that helped even more.

And the thing that finally helped the most was forcing herself to think of the words to a song.

Comin' for to carry me home.

When Lulu was finally able to open her eyes and peek around the tree trunk, it was nearly dark. The Suburban and the tow truck were gone. Hank from the job site was gone. Only Mrs. Rogers and the police were left, and the police looked like they were getting ready to leave, while Mrs. Rogers ranted on, reminding Lulu of angry Aunt Ruth.

Maybe Lulu should stand up, and walk around the tree toward them all and say, "Hi. I'm Lulu Johnson. Are you looking for me?"

But if she did, it would be the real end. She would be sent away, maybe to Aunt Ruth or maybe not. She might be with Serena or she might not. She might be here in this small and cold but pretty darn nice Montana town that she'd come to like a lot, with a handful of people she'd come to like a lot—or she might not.

She might have her wishes come true, or she might not.

Lulu knew things she'd never really known she knew, but there they were, plain as day.

Her daddy had run away that first time for the month when he'd left the girls with Aunt Ruth—and later, he had run away from Texas with Lulu and Serena if truth be told—because if he'd been caught with all those unpaid bills for Mama's care, and caught with all the other stuff that he hadn't tended to when Mama got sick, caught with the things he neglected and dropped because it was all too much trying to care for himself and Lulu and Serena and all the *stuff*—he had run away because if he hadn't run away, he might have been sent to jail.

Yes, he'd also run away because of his sadness, but it was his sadness that had made it impossible for him to stand up and do the right thing, and when people didn't do the right legal thing, they could be sent to jail.

Then they might have been a family, or they might not.

None of this was Lulu's fault, that was true, but she'd seen enough of life to know that adults often don't listen to kids and often do things that makes kids sad, like separating sisters from sisters and parents from children.

No, if she went to the police right there, she might be okay—or she might not.

Breathe in, said Lulu's brain. *You can't find Serena or your daddy if you die.*

Lulu was wearing her warm puffy coat, and she had her

backpack. She stepped away from the tree, stepped into the deeper shadows of the cottonwood trees. She had to find a safe place to be.

First for the night.

Then—and only when she found Serena and her daddy—for forever.

45

Lulu walked up the darkening street. It was Friday night of a holiday weekend. The Main Street of town was lively with people out, even with the cold, because the restaurants and bars were open and the movie theater was playing the latest release.

Lulu did not want to be where there were lots of people, some of whom might recognize her from school, from the laundromat, from the food bank, from the Lutheran church.

Her feet led her on a familiar path down a side street away from the bustle, and before she knew where she was, she was standing in front of the public library.

It was closed, of course. She stood outside staring at it, as if she willed some angel to come winging in to open the doors.

And then, to her everlasting amazement, an angel did appear. Two, in fact. But they didn't wing. Two women pulled into the back parking lot of the library in a rattly old Ford pickup.

Lulu moved around the side of the library, keeping to the shadows.

The two women, housekeepers, Lulu thought, were chattering away as they got out of the truck. One of them had a big ring of keys and she unlocked the back door of the library, and they went inside.

The women did not lock the door behind them and it was an old-fashioned kind of door that didn't lock by itself.

Lulu slipped along the wall to the door, and watched as lights went on in the hallway inside, and then down at the end of the hallway. When she thought the housekeepers were busy collecting their equipment and getting down to business, Lulu opened the door and squeezed inside, closing the door softly behind.

She tiptoed down the hallway in the opposite direction of the lights. The two women continued to chatter as they worked, dusting, vacuuming, cleaning the bathrooms and the staff room, and they made enough noise that Lulu was pretty sure they wouldn't hear her even if she did step on a squeaky board.

Lulu had spent enough time in this old library building to know stuff about it. Like she knew there was a tower that was off-limits to the public, but that could be reached by a stair. Ms. M had shown Lulu the tower one summer Saturday, mainly because she needed to find something up there and Lulu had begged to go with her.

"This is one of the old Carnegie libraries," Ms. M said. "When they built it, they put in this tower with a bell, in case they needed to rally the town to some disaster, like a fire. I've been told that they rang the bell for the last time at the end of World War One, but of course that was in celebration. The bell is gone but you can see a lot of the town from up here."

There were windows on all four sides of the bell tower that used to be open because of the bell, but glass had been installed "to keep the birds and bats out. Otherwise we'd have a real mess in here." Lulu had walked from window to window while Ms. M found what she wanted, the windows looking out over the town, toward the mountains on one side and the river on the other.

Now, in the darkness, Lulu found the door to the tower, slipped inside, slid underneath the chain and the dangling NO ADMITTANCE sign, and climbed to the top. In the tower room there was enough ambient light that she could see.

The small tower room was used for storage of all kinds. There were boxes of brochures advertising the library, a stack of two weeks' worth of newspapers for recycling, posters for special events. There were even a few cartons of books—books that would go in the annual library sale. The floor was wood and creaky-old, so she had to be careful, even if the cleaning women made noise but just in case they got quiet. Though it was a bit musty and almost every surface was hard, it was dry and warm—warm from the heat that rose up the stairwell—and safe, for now.

Lulu found a spot where she could sit with her back against some old stacked shelving. That was when it hit.

Fear. Loss. Helplessness. A terrible, aching loneliness. And a sharp hunger pang that came out of nowhere now that she was safe.

Lulu could do almost nothing about the first four things, but she could deal with the last, so for the moment she buried those four dark things and dealt with her suddenly demanding stomach.

She dug around inside her backpack and found a squished cereal bar. She always carried a water bottle and she had some water left.

Lulu took care of the hunger. But the rest of it—the aloneness, the loss of Serena, the loss of Daddy, the not knowing what to do next—taking care of those was much harder.

46

It TURNED out that the library was a really good place to hide, if you were trying to figure out what to do next when you were in some kind of trouble.

Once the cleaning ladies had gone for the night Lulu could use the bathroom. Safety lights were kept on all night, so she could see where she was going. And she found that there was food in the staff room—cookies and apples. Someone had even left personal stuff in a drawer—toothpaste and a comb, which Lulu planned to use when she woke up.

Up in the tower she took out the stack of her colored paper and began to fold. Folding paper cranes, she'd discovered, emptied her mind. Let her mind rest, much the way slipping inside a character onstage let the world slide away.

Plus, she needed to make a lot of cranes, because she'd lost all she'd made so far, and she still believed, still hoped, was still sure, that if she made those paper cranes, as many as she could, her wishes would come true. Maybe the cranes that were left inside the Suburban counted. She decided they would as long as they were left alone.

By the time her eyes began to close out of sheer weariness, Lulu had made another thirty-two cranes.

But falling asleep was hard, even as her hands kept busy with the cranes, because every so often her quiet mind filled again with feelings. She kept thinking about Serena. She missed her sister's warm back. She wondered whether Serena was scared, or missed Lulu's warm back. Or maybe Serena would be so mad at Lulu she'd never speak to her again.

Lulu was mad at Laurie. She was mad at Daddy. But she was more angry at herself. How could she have been so stupid? So irresponsible? She should have been there. She should have been there for Serena. She should have shown up. She should have done what needed doing.

Because now, being without Daddy, she might never get Serena back again.

It was way late in the dark night before Lulu fell asleep.

And then she woke up while the dawn light was still pale.

Lulu knew she had to leave the next morning as early as possible, and stay out while the library was open, because she couldn't be sure that one of the librarians wouldn't come up to the tower for some reason. She had to hope that she'd be able to get back in and hide again before night.

Lulu went downstairs early in the morning and hid in the bathroom until she heard noises, then slipped outside as the librarians were scurrying around and people were coming for books and events and everyone was distracted.

She'd decided she would try and find the social services office. Just to find out where it was. Maybe she'd be able to gather information, like where kids went when they were taken to social services. Maybe they stayed right there? Maybe they went to the hospital? To the police station? For the moment it was the only thing she could think to do other than walk.

The day was brisk with a biting wind but the sun was out. Lulu felt the cold run right through her even with the puffy coat. The bell tower had been warm, warmer than the Suburban, so overnight she'd gotten used to not feeling the chill.

It was awfully early so she went to the food pantry because she knew it was open, and thought she could find something more to eat, plus get warm.

Most of the food was canned or dried, but there were a few fresh things from time to time. Today they had carrots again. Lulu took a bunch of those plus a couple of juice boxes and a handful of granola bars. She couldn't take anything that might spoil and she could only carry what would fit in her pack.

The man was there, the one she recognized. She tried to avoid him but he saw how little she had taken and stopped her.

"You need help?" he asked, not unkindly.

Lulu put her best new-found acting skills to work. She squared her shoulders and looked him straight in the eye. "Nope." Then she paused. "Maybe you can tell me where the social services office is."

He didn't hesitate. "Corner of Eighth and Main. But they're closed weekends. Holidays, too."

Disappointment flooded Lulu, but she smiled and said, "I figured they would be. Just need to visit them next week. After the holiday."

He nodded. "Good," he said. "Good."

It wasn't good, and she wasn't really sure why he'd said so. But she still smiled, and went on her way, her pack holding her food and all those newly made paper cranes.

The social services building was a low brick structure set in a block of similar nondescript buildings. It was solidly closed. No cars were parked out front. There was no way Serena would be there now. Disappointment surged through Lulu.

Lulu bit her lip. Was Serena scared? Was she lonely and worried? Was she still sick—or worse, even more sick?

Stuck to the inside of the glass in one second-floor window of the building were paper hearts and flowers. Did Serena spend time in that room? Was that where other lost or rescued children spent time, too? Maybe a bunch of children showed up in that building at the same time and Serena had made friends. Or was that room just an office of someone who liked hearts and flowers and therefore must be a nice person who looked after Serena?

Oh, Serena. Lulu thought her heart would break.

This was Lulu's fault. She hadn't done things the right way. Laurie was right. Hiding their predicament wasn't the best way to handle things. She should have asked for help. She should have searched for Daddy even though she didn't know where to begin. Even though she'd thought that would be a bad idea. Even if she'd thought it was hopeless. But she could have asked for help from someone.

No, that was the trouble, wasn't it.

After what happened with Mama, and then with Daddy disappearing that first time, and then with Aunt Ruth, Lulu didn't trust any grown-up enough to ask them for help. That had been the trouble, the trouble that she'd felt for such a long time that it was a part of her.

She felt it since the doctors looking after Mama had let her down.

Since her daddy had gone away that first time and left her and Serena with Aunt Ruth.

Since she'd overheard Aunt Ruth talking about what was to be done with Lulu and Serena.

Since the incident at the drill site.

Grown-ups were not to be trusted, she was sure of it. So she hadn't. She didn't. She wouldn't. It was why she stood up. Why she stepped in. Why she . . .

"Lulu?"

Startled, she whipped around. "Deana?" The last person she expected to see.

"What're you doing here?" Deana asked.

Lulu hesitated. "I was kind of hoping they'd be open. Even though it's Saturday, I was just kind of hoping."

Deana looked past Lulu at the building. "Oh!" Then she said, as if she'd never seen the place before, "Social services. How come?"

"Just . . . stuff. What're you doing here?" Lulu asked back.

Deana shrugged. "I wanted to get out of the house and I just started walking. I got kind of lost in thought."

"Oh."

They stood like that, shuffling on the sidewalk, until Lulu said, softly, "Want to walk to the park?"

The public park was a grassy meadow, now brown and frosty, dotted with almost-bare trees and rough wood picnic tables, and there was a small playground. It was usually quiet because there were so many outdoor places around this Montana town for folks to choose from—streams and mountains and hiking trails and bike paths—but Lulu thought the park was beautiful, even now in the fall with the leaves coating the ground and the chill in the air.

Deana tilted her head as if she hadn't heard right. But then she said, her voice very small, "Sure."

47

By the time they walked the seven blocks from the social services building to the park Deana had started to talk again, chattering as she always did. But she wasn't chattering about clothing or her friends or even their writing stuff. She was chattering about her life.

Deana was an only child. She had a black-and-white cat named Oreo. Her mom was not a great cook, but her dad was. She wanted to be an actress someday, and she loved to sing. She liked to ski in the winter and hoped for lots of snow. She was bored being alone, playing by herself on that Saturday morning so she went for a walk. She'd ended up on the corner of Eighth and Main and there was Lulu.

Lulu listened, and didn't say anything, except, "I love singing, too."

At that Deana chattered on about this music and that

music and how much fun the play at school was going to be.

So when Deana paused—by this time they were sitting side by side on the swings because the playground was empty—and asked, "What about your family and stuff?" Lulu was taken aback.

But then she said, and it surprised her to say, especially to Deana, because it was the first time she'd ever said those words out loud, "My mama died." She paused, and added, "A year ago."

There was a long silence that hung in the air like slow-falling snow. Like leaves, suspended. Then Deana said, her voice a hush, "I'm so sorry."

Lulu took a deep breath. "Thanks."

Then another silence. "What about your dad?" Deana said.

"He's . . ." and Lulu couldn't finish. She waved her hand in the air.

"Yeah," said Deana, with a heavy sigh. "I get it. My dad is hopeless, but so's my mom. Neither one of them really listens to anything I say." She scuffed the dirt with her toe. "Maybe," she said, with a funny note in her voice, "maybe I talk too much and that's why they don't listen."

"My dad does," Lulu said. "Or, when he's around . . ."

"The trouble with dads is they get so busy trying to keep all the balls in the air. Trying to make a living. Trying to make everyone happy. Or that's what mine says."

"Right," Lulu said uncertainly. Was that what her daddy

was doing? Trying to make everyone happy? Out somewhere trying to make a living? Was the work he'd been doing since they got here not enough? Were Lulu and Serena a burden, making his life harder? Is that why he left?

Or did he leave because of the same kind of sadness he'd felt the first time he left? Or . . . had they finally caught up with him, the people in Texas that he owed all that money to, and was he running away from them again?

Lulu's chest tightened. She had to try to breathe.

"You have any brothers or sisters?"

"A sister," Lulu said, and closed her eyes.

"I wish I had a sister. Someone to talk to. I mean, I have friends, but they don't really understand everything because they just . . . don't," Deana finished. "You know?" she said, shyly, glancing at Lulu.

Lulu nodded, swallowing hard. "I know," she whispered.

There was another long silence. The sun was high; it was almost noon. The wind blew and the trees shed more and more leaves, leaves that twirled and turned and danced to the ground around them.

Lulu opened her backpack and reached inside. "I've got carrots. And granola bars."

"Oh!" said Deana. "Cool!"

They each ate one carrot and one granola bar and drank one juice box, and though Lulu knew that would leave her less for later she didn't care.

As Lulu was closing her pack one of the paper cranes flew out. A bright blue crane. It flew out, *swish-boom*, like it needed to fly.

"Ooo!" Deana said. The crane landed at her feet. Then she whispered, "That's so awesome." She bent and picked it up and turned it in her hand. "Did you make it?"

Lulu nodded. Then swallowed. "You can have it."

"You mean it?" Deana looked like she'd never been given something so precious, and that made Lulu happy.

Deana began to talk about the play again, and music, and some of the weight pressing against Lulu's chest eased away. Just to talk about something else. Just to hear Deana chatter on about something else other than family. Just so Lulu could sit still and not talk and try not to think in the warm sun and cold wind and whirling leaves.

The sun slid sideways, toward the west.

Deana said, "I heard you practice."

Lulu stopped swinging on the swing. "What?"

"I was there. When you and Jack practiced before the try-outs. I was thinking of practicing too and so I was behind the curtain and watched you guys." Deana turned the paper crane in her fingers. "I knew then." She paused. "You've got a really great voice."

Lulu swallowed.

Deana stood up. "Listen. My mom and dad are probably

both gone now. Dad is working, and mom has probably gone shopping. You want to come to my house?"

A house. A real house. Did Lulu even deserve to be in a real house? She'd let her mama down. She'd let Serena down. She'd even let her daddy down, because she hadn't looked for him, hadn't searched him out, had, she suddenly realized, just now realized, in some part of her heart given up believing he'd ever come back, and that her standing up was more than important. It was essential. It was the only thing that mattered.

But she'd failed. Serena was gone.

"Okay?" Deana asked, watching Lulu.

"Um . . ." she said.

"C'mon. We can have cookies and I can show you my LOL Fashion Dolls. I'm collecting them all. Do you have any?"

Fashion Dolls? Lulu thought of Serena. "You mean Barbie?"

"The *actual* Fashion Dolls," Deana said. "LOL, of course."

Lulu shook her head. "I don't . . . know."

"Really? Gosh, we've got to find you one, just for you! C'mon, you can look at mine. Decide which one you want to buy. Or, hey. I can give you one to start." She shrugged. "My mom'll buy me another." Deana stood up. She chattered the whole entire walk, all about her dolls, their names and everything and which one she wanted Lulu to have.

When they reached Deana's house, Lulu's breath got stuck in her throat. The house had two stories. It was so long

Lulu couldn't see through the manicured autumn-colored shrubs to the far corner. It looked like something out of Ye Olde England—or the pictures Lulu had seen of Tudor-style cottages—with wood and stucco. The front door was decorated with dried corn and a couple of pumpkins. The back door was decorated by a doll who was supposed to look like a harvesting farm girl, complete with pitchfork.

The whole house reminded Lulu of a fairy-tale princess house.

Lulu stood on the threshold of the back door and stared down the long hallway. It was bright and clean and . . . home.

Lulu had had a nice house once upon a time. A nice home. It was small, way way smaller than this, but it was nice, with its warm yellow globe light. This was something else, something grand, something she'd never even dreamed of living in, and Lulu couldn't.

"Deana. I've got to go."

"Really? You haven't seen my Fashion Dolls collection yet. I wanted to give you Royal Bee."

"Maybe next time."

"Oh." Deana looked at the floor, and shoved her hands in her pockets. The paper crane, sticking out of her coat, slid out silently, winging softly to the floor. Like it wanted to fly again. "Okay. See you next week."

Lulu watched the blue crane. There it lay, on the floor. She was ready to pick it up. Ready to take it back if Deana didn't want it. Deana didn't seem to notice, one way or the other, and that broke Lulu's heart a little.

"Okay," Lulu said, and stepped outside the fairy-tale princess house into the cold, wan sunlight of late afternoon, back into her reality.

48

LULU MADE her way back toward the library. The wind was biting, snaking right through her puffy coat, up the sleeves and down the collar. Her mind twisted like the leaves that whirled around her.

Deana had a home, a nice home. Parents, too. Lulu had nothing now except the pack on her back.

Her daddy had left, for the second time, left her and Serena without a word, left and hadn't come back to the Suburban in which he'd hauled them to Montana and away from the only home they'd ever known. Now even the Suburban was gone and Lulu, walking alone down the sidewalk in a biting Montana wind, shifted without warning from sorrow to anger.

"Sometimes people who are angry are really just scared,"

she had told Serena. Now Lulu thought, *Sometimes people who are scared get really, really angry.*

Lulu stopped in the middle of the sidewalk. She felt like she was one of those instant teakettles and what was inside her went from still to boiling. Even her skin got hot, so hot that she yanked the pack from her shoulders and opened her coat. As she did, a pale gray crane flew out from the top of the pack, landing on the sidewalk among the yellow aspen leaves.

Lulu stared at the crane, her blood boiling, her heart pounding, and then she raised her foot and crushed the crane.

She twisted her foot back and forth, and when she lifted it again, the crane was a gray paper ruin.

Lulu blinked. She swallowed, hard.

The heat inside her simmered, then settled, then lifted into the late afternoon sky, dissipating as suddenly as it had arisen.

Lulu knelt down on one knee on the cold concrete. The crane's neck was broken, its wings shredded. Lulu's heart hurt. She felt like the crane. Broken.

A single sob escaped her before she swallowed the rest.

She touched the gray paper, as if it was a real bird, a baby robin maybe, fallen from the nest, or a cardinal that had smacked into the window as they sometimes did back in Texas. Lulu tucked the tips of her fingers underneath the broken wings.

She lifted it and tried to straighten the wings, but only succeeded in adding another crease.

Lulu handled the crane gingerly and returned it to the pack, laying it on top of the other cranes, snuggling it among them, a tiny hurt thing among colorful wings that gathered around the damaged gray bird, nestling it like a cradle, and Lulu's heart ached.

49

WHEN LULU arrived back at the library, it was near to Saturday closing time. She figured she'd do what she did in the morning—hide in the bathroom until all was quiet and then climb back up to the bell tower.

Only she didn't figure on running into Ms. M.

"Lulu!" said Ms. M, as Lulu was moving through the downstairs sections. "I missed you at the laundromat this morning!"

Lulu turned. Right away she called on those new-found acting skills again. She put on a bright smile. "Hi, Ms. M!"

Ms. M stood still and watched Lulu, a little wrinkle forming between her eyes. "You okay?"

"Oh, sure!"

Ms. M nodded very slowly. "Are you looking for a book? It's almost closing time."

"Oh, gosh, is it? Yes, I need something for the rest of the weekend. Something funny."

"Come with me, then."

Ms. M gave her a couple of choices and Lulu picked one, checked it out, put it inside her pack, and, as she did, another crane flew out of her pack. Like it wanted to fly, too.

This one was orange.

Ms. M said, "Oh!" and bent and picked it up.

Lulu's breath caught.

"This is lovely, Lulu," Ms. M said, and reached to hand it back to her.

"You take it," Lulu said fast. "For good luck."

Ms. M smiled. "Yes. I know that story." Then a strange look passed over her. "Are you making lots of these?"

"Oh, some," Lulu lied. "A few."

Ms. M hesitated. "You sure you want to give this one up?"

Lulu nodded. She'd already decided, after the car, after Deana. If Lulu made the cranes, they counted, no matter where they ended up.

From the back of the library, someone turned out the big overhead lights. Ms. M said, "I guess it's time to go home."

"G'night," Lulu said, and, after another bright smile, made her way outside.

First she walked down the street to the next block, then turned the corner and walked to the end, then turned back to where she could see the library's parking lot. She watched

Ms. M get in her car and drive away. Lulu waited a little longer behind a big old cottonwood, in case. She hugged her puffy coat tight around her chest as the wind began to pick up again, and at last Lulu walked back up the block and around to the back of the library.

Where she waited in the growing shadows. Hoping beyond hope that the cleaning ladies were regular, even on Saturdays.

They were.

50

Lulu let herself sleep late. The stacks of last week's news-papers, spread out, made a pretty decent mattress so once she had fallen asleep—which was hard, again, with all those thoughts about Serena and her daddy and how Lulu had failed everyone and especially herself—but once she fell asleep she actually slept. The library was closed Sundays. And Monday was a holiday so it was also closed then. She'd have the whole place to herself, all day long for two whole days. It felt like a good dream, spending an entire two days in a place filled with books and no one telling her what to do, even if another part of her was trying to figure out what to do and trying not to be afraid.

She discovered an abandoned charger in the break room that fit her iPod perfectly, which was good since she'd left her own charger in the Suburban, so she charged it up, and was able to listen to her favorite music again. She went from room to room, from section to section, exploring books. She pulled books out from the shelves just to see what they looked like inside, things with titles like *New Kid* (because that's what she was) and *My Life As An Ice Cream Sandwich* (because it sounded fun). She spent most of her time in the children's room, reading picture books, one after another.

Lulu found a picture book about sandhill cranes. They mate for life, it said, and could live for thirty years or more. Some summered over in Montana to lay their eggs and raise their young. They flew in great social groups, like Miss Walton had said, and made a distinctive sound when they called. They had wingspans of as much as five feet long and they danced in courtship.

That made Lulu think about Jack, standing with his arms akimbo, and she suddenly felt sick. What would Jack think of her, of her being so irresponsible? What would Jack think of her when he heard she lost her sister? When he heard she lived in a car? When he heard that her daddy left and didn't come back? When he heard that she hid out in the library, which was probably illegal? When he heard that she'd lied to him about almost everything?

Lulu rubbed her cheeks hard because she'd clenched her teeth so tight her jaw ached.

There was no way she'd ever let on to Jack that her life was such a ruin, such a mess, so broken. No. Way. She didn't want

Jack to think of her the way her Texas friends had thought of her after her mama died, like her condition was contagious. She couldn't bear it if Jack looked at her the way her old friends had.

Lulu made batches of paper cranes throughout the day, ten at a time. Ten cranes and then some reading. Ten more and then more reading.

The crushed gray crane went inside a small pocket of her backpack, so that she could protect it.

Lulu and her daddy and Serena had migrated from Texas to Montana just like the sandhill cranes, except when fall came Daddy and Lulu and Serena had stayed in Montana. When maybe, Lulu thought now, they should have gone back to Texas.

Except she didn't want to go back to Texas any longer. Even though she didn't have boots. Even though she wasn't sure about snow and cold. She wanted to find Serena and Daddy—if that was possible, which she wasn't sure of any longer but she still had to try—and stay right here in this town in Montana, surrounded by mountains and rivers and blue, blue sky. If she found Serena and Daddy, no one would ever have to know about the Suburban and what Lulu had done or not done.

She had enough food to satisfy her, at least for today. Monday would be a stretch. Tuesday she would have to go to social services, though it was the last thing she really wanted to do, but she had to because it was the first step in her new game plan. It was the only way she figured that she could find Serena, at least.

It began to snow in the afternoon, and the library felt warm and inviting. All those books. All to herself. The old radiators clanked and hissed as they came on. As the day wore on and it grew shadowy and then dark, Lulu put on her headphones and danced and sang by the glow of the pale safety lights and tried to keep the bad thoughts away, the thoughts about how she'd failed her family. And then she began to make paper cranes again.

She made paper cranes until her fingers ached and her eyes blurred. They piled up around her in her tower nest. More and more and more, as the snow fell softly, silencing the world outside while she was warm and nested inside, her cranes piled up around her like multicolored snow.

When she finally fell asleep Lulu dreamt she was reading one of the last-week's newspapers that lay spread out underneath her.

She dreamt she read an article that she couldn't understand. UNIDENTIFIED read the title. It was a strange story about two men and they were both mixed up with cranes, sandhill cranes flapping their giant wings, dancing, wings akimbo, like Jack.

51

LULU THOUGHT she was still dreaming.

First the light. So bright it was blinding, shining right in her eyes, so when she opened them she couldn't see.

Then the touch. Someone's fingers on her cheek, brushing her hair off her forehead.

Then the realization. The newspaper. The one that lay under her head surrounded by her paper cranes. The article in the paper about two men, one found unconscious, hurt, with no identification by a second man who was alerted by the strange behavior of a sandhill crane. Lulu understood, with a shock, what had happened to her daddy, when the story filtered through her unconscious brain and into waking-ness.

Lulu had been so sure there were no coincidences that it

just hadn't occurred to her that there might be something like coincidences after all.

She sat up with a start in the tower room that was now filled with bright daylight bouncing off snow, and stared straight into the very concerned eyes of Ms. M.

And then, for the first time since she could remember, Lulu began to cry.

52

IT WAS all because of a crane.

Ms. M had been coming into the library on the holiday to catch up on some work when she saw that the tower door was open, and a yellow paper crane lay on one of the steps leading up to the tower, right underneath the chain with the NO ADMITTANCE sign. After seeing it there she had a hunch, she told Lulu.

Well, sure. It was a crane.

She told Lulu this while her arms were wrapped around Lulu, who sobbed. She sobbed and sobbed as if all the not-crying over time had built up a well of tears that just had to come out now, as Lulu sat in a bed of paper cranes with Ms. M hugging her and saying, softly, "There, there."

Lulu sobbed because she'd never make enough paper cranes. She sobbed because of the mistakes she'd made since

Daddy had disappeared. She sobbed because of the things she remembered now about her mama. She sobbed over the loss of Serena, and she sobbed over the crushed gray crane in her pack.

And she sobbed because she was pretty sure she knew where Daddy was now, and why hadn't she thought of this possibility and why had she doubted him, and why she'd thought he'd abandoned Lulu and Serena instead of really truly met with an accident.

Lulu sobbed harder because she had doubted her own daddy. And she sobbed with relief because it looked like he was still alive. Still with her. She hoped.

Lulu sobbed hardest because Ms. M was right there, telling Lulu it would be all right and she'd help with whatever Lulu needed and Lulu hadn't had to ask.

But now she had to stop sobbing and straighten up and get to the hospital right away because she was as sure as sure that the unidentified man who was lying there in a coma was her daddy.

Slowly, slowly, Lulu stopped sobbing, and gulped big gulps of air, and then she sniffed and blew her nose with the tissue that Ms. M gave her. She swallowed hard so that she could speak.

"My daddy," Lulu said, and stopped. She looked up at Ms. M, whose wide brown eyes reminded Lulu suddenly of her mama.

"Yes, honey," Ms. M said, her voice as soft as feathers. "Go on."

Those wide brown eyes and those words made it kind of hard to go on. Because all this time Lulu hadn't gone on with any other grown-ups. She hadn't trusted them enough to go on.

But now Lulu did. She said, "My daddy's been missing. But I think I know where he is."

Ms. M waited. She waited, so still Lulu could see the dust whorls in the air around her head. Lulu whispered, "I think he's in the hospital."

Ms. M said, "Well, if you think that's true, let's go there right now." She stood up and brushed her skirt and held out her hand, and Lulu took it.

Lulu took the newspaper, too, as they went, because she needed to read the article from start to finish, because there was a secret about what had happened to her daddy locked inside those words. She read it out loud to Ms. M as she sat strapped into the back seat of Ms. M's car.

"Strangest thing," said the man who was interviewed in the article. "I'm a veteran bird-watcher, but I've never seen the like. Heard this crane out in the meadow, calling as if her baby had been taken by a fox, so I grabbed my binocs and went out there, and this crane was dancing over something that turned out to be an injured man. Now, if you know cranes, they do dance but it's in the spring, of course, and it's the males that dance. I'm pretty sure this was a female crane. And so late in the season, and all alone. It was like it was her sole purpose to call attention to the poor guy, though maybe it was just that there was a fox and her own baby out there, too."

The article went on to say that the injured man had appeared to have been beaten by someone, maybe looking to rob him, or maybe just because, and the grass was awful high so he'd been hidden and if it hadn't been for that crane and the man with his binocs, why, with the cold and snow, why . . . and the injured man had suffered major trauma and was in a coma, with no identification, and if anyone thought they might know who he was to please call this number.

Ms. M, driving now to the hospital, said, "That story was on the television news yesterday. Someone came forward and said they knew him. Is your daddy a carpenter?"

Lulu thought she might cry again but she held back. Instead she told Ms. M everything. About her mama being sick and how her daddy got so sad. About the money that he owed after her mama died. About leaving Texas for Montana. About living in the Suburban. About her daddy disappearing. About how she hid it when he disappeared. About how it was hard. About how Serena was taken away by social services.

Telling Ms. M everything felt so wonderful it was as if her heart was lifted up, floating, flying.

Partway through Lulu's life story, Ms. M stopped the car by the side of the road and turned right around from the front seat as she listened to Lulu's confession; most of the time Ms. M looked like she was trying hard not to burst into tears herself.

At the end Lulu said, "Can you help me find Serena?"

Ms. M's lips were pursed. She took a deep breath. "I'll try." She paused and shook her head. "I can't believe you were living in your car and you didn't say anything. I wish I could've helped. I wish I would've known. I'm so, so . . ." Her lips grew tight.

Ms. M turned back around and rubbed her fingers over her eyes, and drove on.

It was him.

The room was dark, like Mama's last room, and there were lots of beeps, like in Mama's last room, and the darkness and the beeps pushed the air out of Lulu's lungs again like before and she had to stand in the doorway to slow down her heart so she could breathe again.

So she could stand up.

Lulu moved to the side of the bed and took her daddy's hand. Behind her the doctor began to whisper to Ms. M.

Lulu turned right around and said, "Don't talk behind my back. Tell me." She wasn't going to have that experience this time. Not like Mama.

The doctor raised his eyebrows, but he nodded. "We've kept him in what we call a medically induced coma. We're waiting for the swelling to go down and his injuries to stabilize. It's a way for him to heal. But of course, he couldn't tell us who he was. It wasn't until his boss came in on Friday that we were sure. His boss said he'd been missing since the same day he was discovered in the field, and that him missing work wasn't like him." The doctor paused and looked down at the floor before going on. "And your father's boss said that he put two and two together by thinking it all through from things your father said about where you all might be living. He went to the RV park just as they were towing your car and learned from the park's owner that your family was living in your car. He said that if he'd known your family was living in a car, why, he'd have helped you all out long ago."

Hank, the construction man from the job site, Lulu realized, her daddy's boss, would've helped them. If he'd known. Lulu cleared her throat, and said, "Then, my daddy'll be okay?"

"We believe so. We're doing our best. But it'll be a bit of time before we know everything. It's good he was found so soon after it happened."

Lulu turned back to her daddy. He was so bandaged up, and bruised and swollen, that she might not have recognized him. But it was him and her heart swelled with both sadness and joy.

She'd never known you could be both happy and sad at the same time, but there it was.

She leaned over and kissed her daddy gently on the cheek.

"I've got to go get Serena, Daddy," she said, "I'll be back."

53

Ms. Maurene's husband was a lawyer. He began making phone calls as soon as Lulu finished telling him her story. Lulu stayed at their house, waiting to hear what he learned.

While Lulu waited, Ms. M found some clean clothes from her now college-age daughter that would fit her. She showed Lulu where she could take a shower (which was really nice, a clean bathroom with soft towels and superhot water and nice-smelling soap).

In the shower Lulu let herself cry again because the water felt good and because the heat helped her relax and because she was alone with her tears mixing with the water and because she realized that she hadn't thanked Ms. M for her kindness.

"It's nothing, Lulu," Ms. M said, when Lulu came into the kitchen to a table covered with food and thanked Ms. M over and over. "It's what anyone would do. Should do."

She handed Lulu a plate of peanut butter and jelly and cheese sticks and an apple and then gave her chocolate ice cream. As she ate, Lulu thought. She thought about Ms. M's generosity and that it wasn't what Lulu had ever considered anyone would do. But then she realized that that was partly because she had never asked. And of course not just anyone would, but Ms. M did.

Plus.

Jack had given her his milk when he saw she was thirsty.

Deana had invited her to her home and wanted to give her a doll called Royal Bee.

A strange man had found her daddy beaten and unconscious in the tall grass and called the police.

Her daddy's boss, Hank, had figured out where they lived and then learned about them living in the Suburban, and said he would've helped had he known sooner.

And Ms. M took Lulu in without a second's thought.

So many people cared. So many people wanted to help. Lulu swallowed against the tears that rose in her throat, and realized that she probably wouldn't be someone who didn't cry any longer.

She'd probably be a lot like Miss Walton and cry at every little thing. Cry because people really did care.

"It was tricky because of the holiday weekend but I finally found someone who knew things," Ms. M's husband, Mr. Albert, said, coming into the kitchen and rubbing his forehead as if he had a headache. "Your sister's in a foster care home on the other side of town."

Lulu stood up at once. "I want to go get her."

Mr. Albert said, "Lulu, we can't take her away with us. That's not legal, with your dad in the condition he's in. But you can go see her. And I've arranged for you to stay here until we sort things out later this week."

Lulu bit her lip and swallowed hard. She nodded.

"And while we're on our way there, I want you to tell me everything you know about why your dad left Texas. I'm going to see if I can help straighten things out so when he's well he can get back on his feet."

Mr. Albert had called ahead to the foster family. When they arrived, Serena was waiting on the porch, bouncing from one leg to the other. Lulu jumped out of the car and ran so fast that the two of them collided.

Then Lulu cried for the third time that day.

"They're really nice, Lu," Serena said. "I'm okay. I saw the doctor and he gave me some medicine so my cough is going away. I missed you but I'm all right." She whispered, "They have lots of neat toys. They even have a Barbie with tons of clothes. And they have really good food except they made me eat peas."

Lulu had to laugh through her tears, because she knew how much Serena hated peas.

Serena already knew about their daddy. Social services had

figured things out and had been trying to find Lulu for the past two days. "You were really good at hiding, huh," said Serena, almost proud.

Ms. M said she would bring Lulu back the next day to visit Serena again. Lulu hugged her sister so tight Serena said, "Ow, Lu." But she hugged her right back.

When they drove into Ms. M's driveway, Lulu saw someone out the window.

Jack. He was making a snowman though there really wasn't that much snow and it was already melting.

And she remembered that he lived next door to Ms. Maurene and Mr. Albert.

His eyes were like platters when he saw Lulu get out of their car, and he said, "What're you doing here?"

It was a long explanation that took two glasses of milk—two glasses of juice for Jack—and several cookies each. Jack listened without interrupting so Lulu told him everything, all the way back to when Mama told her about the baby, before she got sick. By the time she was finished, they'd moved to the living room couch and it was suppertime.

Jack stood up to go, but he said, "Maybe while you live here we can practice. Because you'll be living so close to me and all."

"Am I living here?" Lulu said out loud.

From the kitchen Ms. M said, "Yes, you are. You're not leaving until we find you a house to live in. And that's that."

"I can't believe you lived in your car," Jack said, his voice as soft as feathers. "What was it like?"

Lulu had to stop and think. "When we were all together it wasn't . . . like a prison or anything. When the weather was good. But when Daddy . . ." She couldn't finish.

"Nobody should have to live in a car," said Jack, not even sounding a bit like Jack as his face glowed red.

No, she thought. No one should ever, ever have to live in a car. It just wasn't right. No one should have to live without a home.

And then she thought, *No more.*

Suddenly Lulu realized that she would be living in a house again, even if temporarily, with people who cared. Her daddy was alive and would be well, with help. She'd found Serena, who was fine. She could go back to school and be in the play and sing and dance and act with Jack. And she even kind of liked Deana now.

And she'd discovered that many adults weren't so bad after all.

Lulu must have made more cranes than she thought. Because all her wishes were beginning to come true.

54

WHEN LULU went back to school on Tuesday she was in for a surprise. On her desk was a paper crane. But it was a pretty awful crane, clearly made by someone who didn't know how to fold origami.

Or maybe it was deliberately awful, Lulu thought, with a pain that went straight to her heart.

But that wasn't it. Because all day long, more paper cranes kept appearing, and some were terrible but some were really good. One showed up on her desk after she went to sharpen her pencil. Several showed up at the lunch table where she usually sat with Jack. A whole pile were left on her desk when she got back to homeroom. And when she went to after-school—where she saw Serena again, who was still with the foster family but who was back in her routine—the whole room was strung with paper cranes.

Laurie at first pretended she didn't know how it had happened, but then she admitted that she felt so bad for sending Serena with social services and not being able to help Lulu and not knowing that they were living in the Suburban, that as soon as she'd found out everything (because this was a really small town and news like that spread quickly), she and the other girls who looked after the kids in after-school spent their lunch time Tuesday making the cranes hanging in the room and they were all for Lulu to keep.

"But who made the ones today at school?" Lulu asked.

She didn't find out until the next day, Wednesday.

Deana had been really quiet in school. She'd said a serious hello to Lulu—for the first time ever. She'd ignored her old friends—for the first time ever. When she and Lulu did their writing session, Deana read what Lulu had written and said, very softly, "Yeah. That's good."

No chatter. No usual Deana stuff.

At lunch on Wednesday, when Lulu sat down with Jack at their table, Deana ignored her old friends entirely (a couple of whom huffed and raised eyebrows and whispered) and came and sat down next to Lulu. Deana didn't chatter then, either, just talked quietly about the play and how many rehearsals they needed before the performance and how good Jack was at dancing and how Lulu's voice was so pretty.

When they got up to go back to class Deana said, loud

enough for her old friends to hear, "Don't forget I've got a Royal Bee at home for you."

"Oh!" Lulu said.

"I want you to have it."

"Okay. I mean, thank you. Thank you so much."

"Maybe you can come over this weekend," Deana said, and actually sounded kind of shy. She didn't look at the other girls.

That was when Lulu began to think that maybe she and Deana could be friends.

It wasn't until the play rehearsal after school, when Deana sat down next to Lulu in the audience seats while they were watching someone else practice, and handed Lulu another paper crane and started talking, that Lulu figured the rest of it out.

"I had to go on YouTube to learn how to fold them," Deana whispered. "They're hard. Mine are the worst ones. You can tell which."

There was a long silence, filled by someone singing the same verse over after hearing tips.

"How did you know?" Lulu whispered.

"That book we read at the beginning of school. The one about the girl from Hiroshima. I liked that whole thing about the wishes, even though it was really sad."

"Oh!"

Another silence during which Mr. Franzen blocked a scene for two actors.

Deana whispered, "And anyhoo, the story about your dad and you living in the car and everything got all over town real fast once the story broke Monday. And you gave me that paper crane and I put two and two together. So I called around and told everyone else and everybody—well, almost everybody—got down to business making paper cranes, like, all night Monday." She paused. "I can't believe it. The car and all. I'm . . ."

Lulu looked sideways at Deana. Deana was staring straight ahead, at the stage. A single tear rolled down her cheek.

That's when Lulu knew that she would be best friends with Deana. Forever.

55

WHEN DADDY woke up at last, Lulu was by his side. He smiled when he saw her, which the doctor said was a good sign. And while she hugged him and cried a little he said, "Look at you. So grown up," before falling back asleep.

The next day Lulu brought Serena, and he said, "You'll have to tell me how I got here."

But Lulu decided that would wait, and that she would probably never tell him everything she felt while he was missing, because some of what she'd felt was hurtful. Her anger. Her disappointment. Her fear.

But despite that, Lulu thought now that she and Serena and their daddy were lucky, lucky, lucky.

Lucky because they were in Montana, which took care of sick people like her daddy even when they didn't have money.

Lucky because Daddy did get better, even though it took a while and he needed lots of help.

Lucky because Ms. M's husband, Mr. Albert, was a lawyer who could help Lulu's daddy get out of trouble for running away from all those medical bills from Mama's sickness, the bills that he'd left behind unpaid in Texas.

She was even lucky with angry Aunt Ruth, who turned out this time to be more worried than angry, and who, right away when she learned what happened, flew to Montana to look after things with Lulu and Serena and their daddy, even renting a house in town "with my hard-earned retirement money" and staying on until Daddy was out of the hospital, so that Lulu and Serena could live with her instead of being in foster care or burdening Ms. Maurene and Mr. Albert.

"But I don't cotton to this cold weather and this blankety-blank snow," Aunt Ruth groused, after buying the girls winter boots in the shoe store on Main Street. "I'll be getting back to Texas just as soon as your daddy is on his feet again. And why he didn't ask me for more help in the first place I'll never know."

Well, Lulu did know.

Aunt Ruth was so angry when Lulu's mama died that she was a hard person to ask, "Please help," and she didn't seem to want to go out of her way or stand up or take charge or do what needed to be done. In fact, Aunt Ruth had scared Lulu by bringing in the police and child services and talking about sending Lulu and Serena away to foster care.

And that made Lulu realize a couple of things.

First, that Aunt Ruth may have had her own grief to deal with when Lulu's mama died and Aunt Ruth just hadn't been seeing or thinking clearly, and her way of dealing with grief wasn't like Lulu's. Or anybody else's.

Second, that asking for help was as hard for her daddy as it was for Lulu.

But maybe, Lulu thought now, that was foolish, trying to be all strong and in control. Standing up on your own was fine most of the time, but when it wasn't—when you really needed help, when you were down and out—it was okay to ask. Okay to admit that things were hard.

And Lulu also discovered, to her surprise, that lots and lots of people, adults and kids, too, cared. Really cared about almost-strangers like her and Serena and their daddy. Ms. M and her husband cared, of course. But also Daddy's construction boss, Hank, who'd gone to the police after putting two and two together just as the Suburban was being towed and realizing who the unidentified man in the hospital might be. The man who'd found her daddy in the field with the dancing crane cared. The doctors in the hospital here cared. The man at the food bank cared. The Lutherans. Jack. Deana. Laurie.

If Lulu had been in the tower of the Carnegie library and it still had its bell, and she was in trouble, she could pull hard on that bell rope, the sound winging up and down the streets, the people pouring out of houses and churches and shops. And if someone else rang that bell, why, Lulu would be there for them, too.

Come, that bell would sing. And they would.

They would gather in great social groups.

Like the sandhill cranes.

Lulu already knew how to stand up and do what needed doing. It was also good to know when to ring the Carnegie library bell.

56

AUNT RUTH left between Thanksgiving and Christmas, but not before seeing Lulu perform in *Schoolhouse Rock*. She confessed that she "got a little teary because Lulu's sweet voice so reminded me of Athena's sweet voice." And then she added, "And you're quite a little actress."

Lulu got teary herself, thinking that she sounded like her mama, because that meant she carried a little of her mama around with her and it came out every time she sang. And as for acting, it still took her to places far away, and that was wonderful.

Aunt Ruth left for Texas after that because Daddy was home now, in the rental house, and could look after things.

But before she left, Daddy told all of them that he still didn't really know what happened that September morning when he disappeared. All he knew was that he woke really early and began thinking about things. Remembering Lulu's mama. Thinking how bad he'd been to run away, first from the girls—"I'm so sorry, Ruth. I shouldn't have done that to you." And then how sorry he was that he ran away to Montana and didn't face what he had to do with the bills and all, and didn't face his sadness, and didn't do what he should have done to make things right. But he sat in the car that morning and felt so bad that he couldn't fall back to sleep, so he got up to go for a walk and the next thing he knew he was waking up in a hospital bed with Lulu staring down at him.

"I didn't have my wallet, so he got nothing," Daddy said about the man who jumped him, which is what the police thought had happened, though they'd never know for sure. "Maybe that's why he beat me so bad." He paused. "He must have been desperate."

Lulu knitted her hands together, thinking about that feeling.

"Well," said Aunt Ruth, rubbing her eyes. "I've rented this house for a year. I'm sure that'll see you through. But don't you want to come back to Texas with me? It's so gosh-durn cold here."

Lulu looked at Serena, and they both looked at Daddy.

"I think we've found something in Montana," Daddy said, echoing Lulu's thoughts exactly.

. . .

Daddy had been well enough to work on a secret Christmas project for Serena. On Christmas morning, when he unveiled it in the garage, Serena burst into tears.

It was a house.

A dollhouse, of course, but so wonderful that Lulu was awed. It had two stories, and gabled windows, and a front porch and a back stoop, and opened to show three bedrooms and a great big kitchen and living room. The shutters were dark green. The roof was soft brown.

Soft brown like the color of crane feathers.

Like wings.

Lulu stood next to Daddy while Serena went around and around, opening the little doors and windows, and examining the rooms, and talking about how she would do this and that to decorate inside.

Lulu's arm was looped around Daddy's waist and all she could think was how thin he still felt.

"It's a beauty, Daddy."

"Yep," he said. He was silent for a moment. "You really like it?" he asked softly.

"Oh, I do," said Lulu, trying to keep the longing out of her voice.

"Good. Because here's your Christmas present. I talked to Hank"—his boss—"and he's gonna help me build it for real. In that neighborhood you saw. Where I've been working. He'll help me work out the finances."

Lulu bit her lip hard. Sure, she knew now that she could cry, but she didn't want to at the moment. She swallowed and said, "I love it, Daddy. I can't wait."

He squeezed her shoulder, and all she could think was, *Home*.

57

SPRING IS slow to arrive in this part of Montana, Lulu observed. Spring in Montana comes in fits and starts, with unexpected late snows and growing early morning light. But Lulu realized that she liked the cold much better than the heat, which was good now that they were building the house that would be theirs here in Montana, instead of going back to Texas.

Almost every afternoon after school, Lulu picked up Serena and they walked to the new house. Their daddy could only work on it after finishing his regular hours, so the girls would join him and carry lumber or pick up nails or sweep shavings.

Little by little Lulu watched their house grow. She helped make it happen. She and Serena and their daddy.

In the rental house, Lulu had a little table beside her bed, and in the middle of the table she put the broken gray crane, as a reminder.

"That makes me sad," Serena said one night, pointing at it. "You should get rid of it."

Lulu shook her head. "No," she said. "That makes me think."

"About what?"

Lulu didn't answer right away. She was thinking about how it reminded her that it was very easy to become broken and end up living in the back of a car, and that it wasn't anyone's fault but it shouldn't happen, ever. She was thinking that if she could find a way to make it not happen to anyone else, she would, because people deserve better.

But Lulu said instead, "It makes me think about how best to make things right."

58

LULU MET Deana on the front lawn of Lulu's house.

"I'm helping my dad make me a set of bookshelves," Lulu said. She was wearing goggles, pushed up on the top of her head, and gloves, and carrying a hammer. "After which we're going over to work on the Habitat house. They want to finish it for the new family this week, before the cold sets in."

"Cool!" said Deana, propping her bike. "Can I help?"

Serena's laughter filtered down through the open window. The aspen behind the house rattled in the slight breeze. It was still Montana summer warm, and Lulu couldn't quite believe that school would start again in only two weeks.

The Suburban was parked in the driveway next to their daddy's truck. Lulu had wanted him to get rid of the Suburban at first, but then she took a bunch of her paper cranes and strung them up in the back, where they filled the car with color. At some point, he was planning to fix it up and sell it, but he wasn't quite ready yet.

Jack pedaled up the driveway and started talking even before he stopped his bike. "Have you guys heard?" he said. "I ran into Mr. Franzen in the grocery store. Guess what play we're doing in school this year."

The girls waited.

"*Les Mis*! I love that music! And Mr. Franzen said it's gonna be set in today's times, to make it more relevant."

Lulu knew the word "relevant" and she even knew how it was spelled.

"We already know who will be the lead," Deana said, shoving Lulu's shoulder. "You'll be really great."

"What're you guys up to?" Jack asked, looking up at the goggles and back to the hammer.

"Making bookshelves for Lulu's room," Deana said. "And then we're heading over to the Habitat project," she added.

"Excellent. Let's get 'em done."

As the three friends walked up the driveway to the garage, Lulu glanced at the Suburban. The sun was shining from behind, illuminating the cranes that were hung across the back. For one second, she could have sworn the crane wings fluttered, a riot of moving color, as if they were real birds and were so powerful they could lift the whole hunk of metal right off the ground and into the blue blue sky.

Acknowledgments

The idea for this novel was born from a news report. I listened to an interview on *NPR* with the father of a family who were living in their car with three children—despite the fact that both parents worked. I began to wonder what a child would feel, getting up every morning after sleeping in a car, getting dressed in a car, doing homework in a car . . . and wondering especially about a young twelve-year-old girl who would be ridiculed for not bathing or having clean clothes, much less the "right" clothes. I began to imagine Lulu's life.

We should all pay attention to lives like Lulu's. It's far too easy to turn a blind eye, and these desperate families are far too numerous in our world. Any of us, at any time, could be in her family's shoes. It's time to speak up, to speak out, and to act.

I ended up writing Lulu's story in a rush, in one month, a rare thing and a gift, and for that I thank the muse and the universe and Lulu herself.

My critique partner and first reader is Jen Cervantes, and I cannot thank her enough for her wisdom, support, and encouragement. She prompts me always to write more deeply. Gracias, otra vez, mi amiga.

My agent, Erin Murphy, who loved this story from the start, is my second reader and critiquer and ultimately my champion in all things. Thank you, Erin. My editor at Simon & Schuster, Krista Vitola, is smart and kind, and I thank her so much for helping me polish this little novel, and for finding the perfect title for it too. When I saw the cover designed by Lizzy Bromley, with the illustration by Henry Cole, I began to cry, it was so beautiful. And in a perfect mind meld, Krista and I each had the vision of seeing Lulu and Serena walking hand in hand, just as Henry has depicted them.

I must acknowledge my wonderful Viking editor Kendra Levin, now with Simon & Schuster, who read this manuscript first and placed it in Krista's more than capable hands.

Many thanks to Morgan York, Chava Wolin, Gary Sunshine, and Kathy Smith.

And lastly, I want to thank my husband, Jeff, who has been my pillar of strength for these many, many years, always supporting me and my work. And my son Kevin, a talented writer and deep thinker, prompts me to question my assumptions, and in that way he has led me straight into Lulu's heart.